"A girl and her dog sit eating salty liquorice
on a half-built suspension bridge in the
Amazon rainforest."

No, wait a minute, that's no way to begin a
story. Let's take it from the beginning and
start with the first chapter.

1

One clear starry night on the cusp of winter, the moon could be seen rising above the rooftops with an expectant smile. It had come far and was full of anticipation, for it was now that the story of the girl and the dog would begin.

☙

The girl was called Elise. She lived with her dad in Mysundegade, where the sun rarely shone, and so they made their own light.

They were up on the roof – where there was a barbeque, two wicker chairs, an old telescope and a view of the whole city and half of space – grilling sausages and roasting chestnuts.

Elise's dad was explaining that no one knew how old the stars were, and that Saturn, Mars and Pluto were just as mysterious as the rest of the universe, and to this Elise said she wanted a dog.

"A dog?" asked her dad. "I thought we were talking about stars."

Elise had her mum's old winter coat on, and there was a bag of liquorice sweets in her pocket. Her dad reminded her they only ate things like that on Fridays. Elise said the liquorice she had in her mouth was from last Friday.

Her dad shook his head.

"Let's see if you can find Cassiopeia."

Elise pushed the telescope away.

"You can't see anything through that old piece of junk, and I'd rather talk about a dog. I'm thinking a girl dog with a soft belly and nice floppy ears."

Her dad said it would be too difficult to have a dog on the fourth floor, never mind the fact that a dog cost a lot of money, and if there was something he didn't have, it was a lot of money. He also said that if he did have a lot of money, he'd spend it on a new telescope.

Elise was well aware that her dad didn't earn a lot from playing the violin at weddings and funerals – and sometimes outside Illum department store.

"And besides," said her dad. "I'd prefer we were able to afford a little frivolity."

Elise shoved her hand in her pocket and pulled out another piece of liquorice.

"I'm pretty sure I could do without frivolity if I had a dog."

Her dad took the sweet bag and said no one bought a dog without giving it careful thought first.

"We bought the red sofa without giving it careful thought," said Elise, "and it's the best sofa in the world for jumping on."

"A dog's a living creature," said her dad, "and it needs care and love, and don't forget you need to walk a dog, unlike a sofa – which by the way you shouldn't be jumping on."

"But couldn't we get a second-hand dog?" asked Elise, knowing her dad had bought a second-hand bike.

Elise's dad started to gather up the food.

"I think I've said all I need to say on the matter, and besides, it's your bedtime and I want to watch something important on channel 6."

Elise said she wouldn't be able to sleep until her dad had promised they would at least go and look at a dog. After all, it didn't cost anything to look. Elise and her dad often went into the Magasin department store just to look.

Elise's dad unbuttoned his coat.

"Look. I'm wearing my old Liverpool shirt, and I have two beers in the fridge, one for each half. I don't know anything about dogs, couldn't tell a Labrador from an air mattress, and right now, I know a young lady who needs to hit the hay."

Elise grabbed her dad and fished the bag of liquorice out of his pocket.

"I'll take care of the dog. I'll walk it and train it so it doesn't chew the table or eat your slippers. Maybe we could get one that has red hair like you. Wouldn't that be nice?"

"Don't think I didn't see what you did with the sweet bag. Give it here."

"The dog can stay in my room – you'll never see it. Dad, I swear on Great-Grandad's grave."

"Your great-grandad's alive and well."

"I meant Great-Great-Grandad's grave."

"Say goodnight to Cassiopeia."

Elise's dad opened the door to the kitchen stairs.

Elise positioned herself in front of him.

"And hello to a dog."

"No, and that's final, and when I say that's final, you know I mean it."

2

Potifar's Pet Salon was located between a grill and a shop where you could get fake nails. Elise had often stood outside peering in through the window of the shop, where you could get your dog's hair cut, its nails trimmed and its teeth cleaned. There were lots of dog baskets, tins of dog food and small reflective vests for dogs to wear in the dark. You could get everything you needed in Potifar's shop, which also sold dates, spices and cheap watches.

Potifar was a large man in a dirty white undershirt who always sat in an armchair outside the shop talking to the people walking past. Today was the same. He struggled to his feet and held out his hand to Elise's dad.

"Welcome to my shop. What's your name, friend?"

"I'm Anders, Elise's dad."

"And I'm Ali Potifar. Might I interest you in a classic watch from Bulgaria?"

Elise prodded Potifar's arm.

"We want to see a dog."

Elise's dad said his daughter had chosen her words very carefully: they hadn't come to buy a dog, just to look at one.

Potifar smoothed his comb-over.

"In my shop, you'll find all you could ever want, and a pretty girl like you might be interested in some bracelets I just got from India that change colour depending on your mood. They're called the caliph's magical rings."

Potifar had already put a bracelet on Elise's wrist.

"See, it's turned red – that means you're happy! But if you feel down and upset, the bracelet changes colour to blue. Only nine kroner... two for eighteen."

Elise repeated that she'd come to see a dog.

Potifar took Elise's hand and showed her around the shop, which smelled of coffee, dog food and Potifar's lunch.

"This," he said, "is the animals' domain. I love animals. Everything that walks on four legs is a friend to Potifar. Here we have a small stuffed cat."

"Who on earth would stuff a cat?" mumbled Elise's dad. Potifar's brother-in-law, apparently.

Elise looked around, but couldn't see any dogs, not even a second-hand one.

"You don't have any dogs, do you?"

Potifar hiked up his trousers.

"My animals need a lot of fresh air. I look after and care for them as if they were my children. In fact, I love them so much I'd rather not sell them, but I'll make an exception for Elise and Elise's dad."

Potifar pushed a curtain of plastic beads aside and bowed.

"Welcome to the animals' paradise."

🐾

In his backyard, Potifar had a wooden shed without a roof, or rather, the remainder of the roof was still there, but since it was only a few planks, it was more accurate to say it didn't have a roof.

Potifar said the animals liked it better that way.

"They sit in the sun and enjoy the fresh late-summer air. All my animals have ruddy cheeks."

Potifar opened the door to the animals' paradise.

"Allow me to give you a free tour – no paying! – starting with Svetlana, who's three years old and a jewel of her species. Svetlana's having a siesta right now, but otherwise she's a lovely little pot-bellied pig with a positive and welcoming nature. She's on offer this week."

Elise stared at the pig lying farting in the hay. Elise's dad said it reminded him he needed to phone his financial advisor.

"Svetlana," explained Potifar, "isn't fussy. She eats what's put in front of her and sometimes a little more – in fact, she ate my braces."

Elise asked him where the dogs were.

Potifar moved on to the next cage.

"Patience, my friend. Here's Hannibal, a successful cross between a pure-bred boxer and a prize-winning king poodle."

Elise's dad asked whether it was an optical illusion or actually the case that Hannibal had no teeth.

"Ah, his teeth," said Potifar, "have unfortunately fallen out, but Hannibal is a magnificent dog and great with children – after all, he can't bite, only suck."

Elise's dad said that of all the animals he'd seen in Potifar's shop, he was leaning towards the stuffed cat.

Elise looked around.

"But is that all there is to the animals' paradise?" she asked

Potifar flung his arms open wide.

"On Wednesday, I'm getting a puppy from Gammel Køge Landevej, perfect for a sweet little girl. What do you say to that, Elise?"

Elise didn't respond, just looked into a dark cage holding an animal that wasn't much bigger than a rabbit, though it wasn't rabbit. If it was a dog with a rotund body and four spindly legs. Its fur was short and white, and its ears were on the side of its head, one sticking out in one direction, and the other in the opposite direction. But the strangest thing about it was its mouth, which – hadn't she known better – was smiling at Elise.

"Look, Dad," said Elise, "it's smiling at me."

"I expect it's got a bellyache," said Elise's dad.

Elise asked Potifar what kind of dog it was.

Potifar's chin dropped onto his chest.

"There was a terrible traffic accident. As you can see, he has a tag that says Gasværksvej, because that's where it happened. I think it was a cement mixer that ran him over."

Elise's dad said it took the word mongrel to a whole other level. Elise asked if she could go into the cage and pet the small dog, and Elise's dad said he honestly saw no reason why she should, but Elise had already opened the door and was crouched down next to the dog, which was doing his best to look cute.

Potifar said that unfortunately he didn't know what breed Gasværksvej was, and Elise's dad said he'd seen dust bunnies that were more pure-bred.

"Is he expensive?" asked Elise.

Potifar sighed.

"I've actually spent a lot on him – he really looked awful when I got him. But since it's you, Elise, you can have him for a hundred kroner including a dog bowl, a bracelet from India and the pill bottle."

"The pill bottle?" asked Elise's dad.

Potifar explained that due to his asthma the dog needed to take a small red pill every day. He could do with being looked over by a vet too, but that was up to them.

Elise's dad pulled Potifar into a corner of the animals' paradise.

"Alright, mate," said Elise's dad, "I know nothing about pets, so I don't know what it is you have sitting in that cage, but I wouldn't take that thing home if you gave me five hundred kroner, ten pill bottles and the caliph's red crakows."

Potifar turned and looked at Elise, who was standing with Gasværksvej in her arms.

"Dad," she said, "he's the sweetest dog in all the world."

3

Something utterly wonderful and completely inexplicable had happened, which was why Elise was at the small park where dogs were welcome as long as they were kept on a lead. There was a slide for children, five chairs for elderly people and a bench for the people drinking beer.

The bracelet Elise had got from Potifar had turned green, and according to the caliph that meant she was somewhere between happy and sad, but in truth, she was utterly confused. The bracelet should have been red really, since she'd finally got what she wanted more than anything, a dog that was sitting nicely and looking around at the other dogs with their noses in the air.

Elise had had the second-hand dog for five days, and for those five days he had been a real angel.

Elise's dad had said that for thirty-nine kroner and a yellow lighter they'd got a well behaved dog that neither howled at the moon nor peed on the carpet, and which answered to his name whether you shouted Gustav, Ditlev or Marmalade.

The dog had a cardboard box from Irma with a picture of plum tomatoes on the side, but now it contained an old pillow for the dog to sleep on, and from the first day, he'd lain down to sleep as soon as the light was turned out, and apart from the fact that he snored so loudly Elise's dad had to sleep with earplugs in, he was civility defined.

The first night, Elise had had trouble falling asleep. Her dad was walking around singing to his plants in the living room. That was usually a good sound to fall asleep to, and Elise had lain down and closed her eyes while thinking about what to call her dog, and perhaps she'd fallen asleep, but it was just then that the inexplicable happened. There was a honey-gold full moon in the sky illuminating much of her room, and Elise could remember asking her dog whether he liked the name Ditlev. Then she'd heard a hoarse voice say something or other, and the voice came unmistakably from the cardboard box... but it couldn't have, and when Elise woke up the next morning, she was sure it had all been a dream.

❧

On the way home from the small park, Elise stopped by the shop that sold black and white film posters, old maps of the world and faded comic books. The old map showed the countries Mesopotamia, Persia and Siam, but since none of those names were suitable for a second-hand dog, Elise decided her dog would be called Prince Valiant the Great. Or perhaps just Valiant. It was important to consider her options carefully, because once the dog had a collar and tag, she wouldn't be able to change her mind.

❧

Elise was going to be home alone that Sunday afternoon because her dad was playing at a wedding in Søndermarken. Elise had waved goodbye to him as he'd cycled off with his top hat and violin case.

There were a lot of things you could do when you were home alone, but Elise spent most of the time sitting next to the model she wasn't supposed to touch in the dining room. It was a scale model of a suspension bridge made of tiny, carved sticks and a lot of fine thread. The model had been made by Elise's mum, who was in the Amazon rainforest making sure the work to build the full-size bridge was going according to plan. Elise wasn't always able to keep from touching the model, and on one occasion she'd missed her mum so much that she'd stamped on and twisted it, but mostly she was proud her mum could build such a big bridge, and in any case, her dad had managed to repair the model again. Elise's mum had been in the rainforest for almost nine months, because you couldn't build a bridge overnight, but on Elise's birthday she'd rung up and said that when the bridge was finished, she'd come home in a bright yellow plane with the Brazilian flag on the wing, and Elise's drawing of the yellow plane had hung over her bed ever since.

Elise sat down in front of the TV to watch

cartoons with a bowl of cornflakes, which she always had with chocolate milk when she was home alone. The second-hand dog sat next to her, also watching the cartoon. Elise put her arm around it.

"I had a dream last night," she whispered, "that you could talk. I heard it so clearly, even though I know you can't. Your legs are bent and your ears stick out weirdly, but you're the sweetest dog in the world, and soon you'll have a name."

Elise's dad had said that all dogs in Denmark had to have an ear tattoo, but that he bet the second-hand dog didn't. But he was wrong, because there was a blue tattoo in its left ear, and even though Elise's dad thought it strange that it said *Highland Park, 47%*, Elise couldn't care less because to her a tattoo was a tattoo, no matter what it said.

Elise put her arm around the dog again.

"I've decided you're going to be called Prince Valiant the Great. You can still have a good name even if you've been in the wars, and Prince Valiant is a great name for a clever, brave dog. I'll just go get some water so we can

christen you properly, like when I was christened at St Matthew's Church in the name of the Holy Ghost."

※

Half an hour later everything was ready for the christening, but something was missing. Specifically, some scented water, so Elise went down to the first floor where Miss Martini lived. To tell the truth, Miss Martini wasn't really called Miss Martini, but Miss Martinsen. Miss Martini was just what Elise's dad called her because she always smelled of sweet Martini. Miss Martini had decorated her flat with a red carpet, huge china dogs, elegant fans and smelly incense sticks. Sometimes she wore a black wig and spoke real Chinese, but that was only when she'd overindulged. Otherwise she folded the most beautiful roses made of the finest silk paper while listening to old Jim Reeves records.

Elise went into the Chinese flat, which she knew like the back of her hand.

"I need some scented water for my dog."

Miss Martini was wearing a red silk robe and a pair

of pink slippers, but had to fumble her way along the wall because she had her black headache glasses on.

"I didn't know you had a dog. What kind's it?"

"He's a second-hand dog," said Elise. "I don't think he's got a kind."

Miss Martini turned around, stretched out her arms and walked into the doorframe.

"Do you really think he'll scent drinking water?"

"You mean drink scented water," said Elise. "It's not for him to drink, it's to christen him. He needs a name, after all."

Miss Martini took off her sunglasses and looked up at the ceiling with a dreamy expression.

"What about calling him Kai?"

"Kai?"

"Yes, Chiang Kai-shek, he was a marvellous man. I can't remember what Kai did in China, but I think it had something to do with rice. I love rice."

Elise said that Chiang Kai-shek was a strange name and that her dog was going to be called Prince Valiant the Great, and that she'd come to get something she could use as holy water.

Miss Martini said all she had that smelled sweet was what was in Mao's mausoleum, meaning her drinks cupboard, and that was how Elise's dog came to be christened using white vermouth.

❧

To mark the momentous occasion, Elise had put on her mum's explorer's helmet. Around her shoulders she wore a silk shawl, and around her neck hung her grandma's necklace made of mussel shells. On her feet Elise wore her Aunt Fie's heels, which were four sizes too big for her, but they suited the occasion. Her aunt had also given her a bright red lipstick, which she'd applied using a – as Fie would say – round hand.

Russian choral music could be heard from the living room. Elise had spent a long time choosing the right music, and since a christening was something quite serious, she'd chosen a solemn male choir from St Petersburg. Her dad had told her that the music had been composed by a man called Rachmaninoff, and that he knew a lot about choral singing and homesickness.

Seven small candles burned on the kitchen table, or not really candles, since Elise wasn't allowed to light candles. Instead she'd collected all the bike lights she could find, new and old, and positioned them in a circle.

Elise turned off the main light.

It was time for the christening ceremony.

Elise lifted the dog up onto the kitchen table, brought her hands together and listened to the singing, which filled the entire flat. Of course, she didn't understand Russian, but her dad had told her it was church music, so it wasn't inconceivable that the fat men were singing a psalm about a second-hand dog being christened.

Elise put a drop of water on the palm of her hand and let it drip down over the dog's head.

"I baptise you in the name of my mum, Potifar and Aunt Fie. From this day on you'll be known as Prince Valiant the Great."

The second-hand dog smiled.

"But my real name's McAduddi," he said.

4

Elise had made a cave under her duvet where she could sit with a torch, as she had so often before when her dad thought she was sleeping. He had been so exhausted from playing the violin that he had collapsed onto the red sofa without getting changed. He was lying on his back with a silly little smile on his face and his violin bow resting on his chest.

Elise looked at her bracelet, which had turned purple. She didn't know what that meant, but she knew how she felt. She felt torn, but it was wonderful. That's why she was sitting in the cave, because it was like there was a bubble bath deep down inside her. She hardly dared move because of all the bubbles. Exactly ten hours had passed since she'd christened her dog Prince Valiant, and in all that time she'd not said a

word to him. He had actually slept for most of that time, but now he was sitting up in his box looking at the moon. Elise gave him a pensive look. Her mum had once told her that when building bridges, the bridge materials need to be carefully tested to make sure they can take the strain in real life. This was probably the case for dogs too. Elise and her dad had bought the dog on a whim, after all, without knowing whether he was housebroken, would tolerate a lead or had lice. So it was high time Elise thoroughly investigated the dog.

"OK," she said. "Here I have a book, your pedigree, which tells me what you can and can't do. We'll start with the paw test. I assume you know where your paws are, but if not, they're at the ends of your legs. Question 1: can you give me your paw?"

The dog didn't react.

Elise picked up her pencil.

"You can't give me your paw. We'll mark that as a no. Question 2: can you sit when told?"

No reaction.

Elise nodded.

"I didn't expect you to be able to do that either. Another no. Now we'll test your hearing, which starts with me clapping my hands to see how you react."

Elise clapped her hands.

The dog gave her an inquisitive look.

"OK, I'll put you down as deaf, maybe only partially."

Elise turned her torch on and shone it in the dog's eyes.

"They say your soul can be seen in your eyes. I'm not entirely sure what a soul is, but I think it has something to do with who you are inside. What I'm looking for in your eyes is a glint of the intelligence that many dogs are born with, but apart from your right eye looking one way and your left eye the other, I can't see the slightest sign of intelligence. It's like looking into the eyes of a hamster."

A terrifying thought struck Elise. What if he wasn't a dog at all, but a hamster? That might explain why he hadn't given her his paw.

Elise gripped the dog.

"Finally, we'll test your speech. You claim, however strange it sounds, that you have a name. We need to test that too, so listen up, because it's your master who decides what you're called. If you can speak, repeat after me: my name is Prince Valiant the Great."

The dog straightened up.

"My name's McAduddi the not-so Great."

Elise pressed her lips together. This was insane – simply insane.

"So you refuse to be called Prince Valiant and claim your name's McAduddi?"

"Or just Duddi. Question 1: can you say Duddi?"

"Riiiight, let's not do that."

Elise swung her legs out of the bed and started to pace around the room, ending up in a corner, where she pressed her forehead against the wall as she counted very slowly and very clearly.

"Dogs," she said, "can't talk. I need to say that out loud. Dogs can bark and growl and howl, but they can't talk."

The second-hand dog jumped out of his box and

pressed his forehead against the wall.

"I disagree. I seem to be talking just fine."

Elise stared at him.

"Don't tell me you're talking just fine – give me an explanation! I've known loads of dogs: poodles, boxers, schnauzers and greyhounds and ones my dad calls a mixed bag, and none of them could say a single word, because if they could have, they'd probably have ended up on TV as the greatest sensation in the world, especially if they'd been bought for under forty kroner in a shop that also sold dried oregano."

The dog raised its head again.

"Just as there's a difference between people, there's a difference between dogs, and I wouldn't rule out finding a puppy in Hvidovre that can say woof."

Elise clenched her teeth. There were so many bubbles inside her now that she couldn't stand still.

"I'm warning you, if this is a cheap trick you learned from Potifar, you can cut it out right now. Then we'll go get our money back, or at least half of it."

"As you wish," said the dog. "I don't mind barking

or growling. In fact, I'm rather good at growling."

"OK," said Elise. "Where did you learn to talk?"

"In Tobermory."

"Tobermory? Is that in Vesterbro?"

"It's a town in Scotland."

"In Scotland? So you're Scottish?"

Elise rolled her eyes.

"When did you learn to talk?"

The dog smiled.

"My mum gave me the gift of the gab before she went to Aberdeen."

"Aberdeen? What's Aberdeen?"

"It's just something us dogs say. When it's time for Grandad to die, we say he's off to Aberdeen. The band with drums and bagpipes follows, but don't you worry your head about that, lassie."

"Lassie?" asked Elise. "My name's not Lassie."

"Lassie," said the dog, "means girl in Scots. It's the same as when you call someone love, hon or sweetie – and you're a bonnie wee lassie."

"I'm not your love, and I'm definitely not lassie."

Elise stomped out into the bathroom, where she sat on the toilet with her arms crossed. The lengths she'd gone to, finding bike lights, Russian choir music and white vermouth, only for that bow-legged mutt to tell her what was what? *I don't want to be called Prince Valiant, and I'm from Scotland, and you're Lassie.* He sure as hell wasn't the kind of dog she'd wanted. If she'd wanted a Scottish dog she'd have bought one, and besides, you don't expect a dog that cost thirty-nine kroner to start talking.

Elise stomped back into her room. Clearly, she had a lot of thinking to do.

"I'm going to bed now," she said, "but there's something I need to say to you, McAduddi, or whatever your name is: we need to agree that we keep the fact you can talk between us. No parading around the neighbourhood boasting about it, and not a word to my dad."

The dog giggled.

"He seems a nice old man."

"Did you just call my dad an old man?"

"A nice one."

"He is *not* an old man."

"What can I say? The man knits his own socks and rubs scented lotion into his hands."

Elise closed her eyes.

"My dad has dry hands. His fingertips are callused from playing the violin, and you don't say a word about his socks, his lotion or his Hardanger fiddle, understand?"

"Yeah, yeah," said the dog. "I got it."

"Don't say you got it, say you understand. I make the decisions here."

The dog told her he'd noticed.

Elise nodded.

"Get settled in your box."

The second-hand dog sat in his cardboard box.

"It's time," he said, "to show the moon our appreciation, and that's best done with a song."

The dog cleared his throat:

> *Oh, lovely maiden, cry no more*
> *For I have returned from the sea*

I'll never leave you; no, never more
not as long as there's whisky.
Oh, lovely maiden, I'm no longer erring
for I have returned from the sea
Living only on salted herring
and on that marvellous whisky.

Elise shook her head.

"What was all that about?"

"It's a sea shanty."

"About whisky?"

"About the best malt whisky there is: *Highland Park, 47%.*"

"Never heard of it. But that's how it is when you always buy what's on offer. Let's sleep. No more sea shanties. Tomorrow's going to be a busy day. I'm meeting my Aunt Fie for brunch. Goodnight and sleep well, Duddi."

"You too," said the dog. "You too, lassie."

Silence descended on the room in Mysundegade, where the moon shone on the Amazonian bridge and the cardboard box containing the second-hand dog.

5

Elise and Fie had their roller skates on. They were standing in Valdemarsgade wearing kneepads and helmets. Fie looked at her stopwatch and counted down from ten, and then it was full pelt to Granola, a coffee shop on Værnedamsvej.

Værnedamsvej was jam-packed with nice shops, five thousand pedestrians and just as many cyclists, and that was just how Elise liked it. Racing Aunt Fie was the second best thing in the world. The best thing in the world was eating brunch with her. Sometimes they went out to Ramses Venner in Vanløse, and other times they skated over to Alice Baba in Østerbro. Fie knew all the coffee shops, and in some places she even had a regular table. She went nowhere without her mobile and computer, and when she

wasn't talking to Elise, she was busy answering texts.

Fie always started by telling Elise her skating was too bold, too fast and too dangerous, and then, before Elise managed to say Fie was just a sore loser, Fie would ask how life was treating her in Mysundegade.

Elise didn't have anything against the question, but she always took a big gulp of her strawberry milkshake before asking her aunt to turn off her computer, put her phone in her pocket and listen well.

"I got a dog."

"Yes," said Fie. "I heard. Apparently, it's small and fat and smells like cheese. How's momma's bridge coming along?"

Fie called all mothers momma. She said she'd seen a photo of momma in the jungle and she'd looked super tough.

Elise leaned in across the table.

"Do you know much about Scotland, Fie?"

Fie said she'd spent two years at university in Dublin, so she knew all about Scotland.

"OK," said Elise. "Switch on your computer and

find a town called Tobermory."

Fie smiled.

"Is it a real place?"

"That's what I need you to find out."

Fie typed it into her computer.

"Bingo," she said. "There is actually a small town in Scotland called Tobermory – where did you hear of it?"

Elise bowed her head and closed her eyes. So it did exist.

"Can you look into what it means when a dog says someone's off to Aberdeen?"

Fie leaned across the table, suddenly grave.

"You're asking weird questions today, Lissi."

"But can you look it up?"

"I don't need to. It's from an old TV series about a sheepdog called Billy who says in the last episode that it's time he was off to Aberdeen, and he means he's about to, you know, die."

Elise finished her milkshake.

"I can't take anymore," she said, sighing.

"That's the first time I've heard you say that about a milkshake."

Elise said it had nothing to do with the milkshake.

"Can you keep a secret?" she whispered.

Fie said she'd never broken a promise when it came to a secret.

Elise looked around and lowered her voice.

"My dog told me."

"Told you what?"

"All that stuff about Scotland and Aberdeen. He said his mum said she was off to Aberdeen just before she died."

After that, Fie ordered a double espresso for herself, another milkshake for Elise and two chocolate croissants.

"I hope you're not making fun of your youngest aunt. You've said weird things before, after all. Remember that time you said you were invisible on Thursdays? Or what about that Easter you told the whole family you were learning to fly but that your wings hadn't developed properly yet?"

Elise rolled her eyes.

"OK, so maybe I made that up, but I'm not making up the thing with the dog. You're the only person who knows apart from Miss Martini on the first floor, but she's got a memory like a sieve, and of course I've written to tell mum, but she's on the other side of the world and has other things to think about. I haven't told anyone else though, not even Dad."

Fie sipped her coffee.

"Maybe I'm being a bit slow on the uptake, but what haven't you told him?"

Elise clenched her teeth.

"That McAduddi can talk."

Fie leaned back and stretched.

"I once had a cat who could dance the ballet. As soon as you put a tutu on him, he'd rise up onto his tippy toes and dance the Dying Swan."

Elise could feel her face turning red. She was absolutely furious. She'd always had a temper, but over time she'd got better at controlling it. Not that she liked controlling it, but she'd much rather do that than hold her breath until she was blue in the face. But not this time.

"Look at it again," she said.

Fie put on her glasses and studied the menu.

"What about it, sweetheart?"

Elise took the menu out of Fie's hand.

"Look up Tobermory, *sweetheart*. I bet Tobermory's a town where a lot of fishermen live, or more accurately, whalers. That's what they make a living from in Tobermory."

"Is that what your dog told you?"

"Yep."

Fie looked it up on her computer and drummed on the table with her long red nails, smiling sourly at Elise.

"So you have a dog from Tobermory. And he talks."

"And sings."

"Ah, he sings too? I also heard he was run over by a cement mixer and cost the same as four hundred grams of diced veal and pork."

Elise said that was true. The dog had been cheap.

Fie took her purse from her coat pocket.

"I have a yoga class in half an hour, but I promise I'll think about what you've said. There's nothing cooler than a dog that can talk, and when I was your age I was best friends with an alligator from Mølleåen."

"So you think I'm lying."

Fie put her credit card on the table.

"I think you got a dog who's small and fat and smells like cheese, and when you got it home it leapt up onto the window sill and sang Silent Night."

Elise adjusted her helmet.

"Wrong," she said. "He sang a sea shanty about a whisky called *Highland Park*."

Fie stared into space.

"*Highland Park?*"

Elise nodded.

"47%."

✿

When they were standing outside the coffee shop, they found it had started to drizzle, but there were still a lot of people milling about.

Fie sighed.

"I don't know whether this is something you've made up or whether you really have a dog that can talk. I have to say it sounds very you, but it was smart not to mix your dad up in it. He's confused enough as it is."

Elise grabbed Fie.

"It's just so hard knowing you don't believe me."

Fie put a hand on Elise's shoulder.

"I didn't say that. I'll keep an open mind. And I feel I should tell you: when I lived in Dublin, I sometimes felt homesick, and for lack of anything better to do I sometimes had a stiff drink, a whisky, and it was always *Highland Park*, but only one, because as you say, it's 47% proof."

❧

Elise and Aunt Fie rolled up Frederiksberg Allé, where the linden trees had shed the last of their leaves. The day was black and white, and Elise's bracelet was green.

6

The girl in the mirror had her tongue poking out of her mouth. She was so dissatisfied with what she saw that she closed her eyes, took a deep breath and held it. In the past, Elise had on occasion been known to get so angry that she would hold her breath, and when during her fourth birthday at Tivoli amusement park her dad had said that she was too little to go on the rollercoaster, she'd held her breath for so long that he'd driven her to the emergency room.

That wouldn't be necessary today, though she was furious she didn't look scary enough. She'd painted her face white and there was a rubber axe in her forehead that she'd bought in a shop called A Thousand Horrible Things, but she still didn't think it was enough. She'd considered blackening her tongue, but her dad didn't think they had any black paint, so he'd suggested buying a bag of Haribo pirate coins, because they always turned your tongue black. Elise wasn't against the notion of eating pirate coins all evening, but it was still a bit too childish. She wanted to be scary, unrecognisable, a vampire who'd just crawled out of their grave, but now she was standing in Mysundegade looking like a prize plum.

In the living room, her dad was playing his violin so it sounded like a rusty old door opening slowly. He said it was a sound he'd had a lot of success with when he performed as a clown at children's birthday parties.

Elise sat on the window seat and looked out at the street. They were waiting for Aunt Fie to collect them in her car.

For as long as Elise could remember, they'd celebrated Halloween in Odsherred, where Elise's grandma lived in an old windmill. There were to have been six of them at the party: Elise, Elise's dad, Aunt Fie, Grandma, Elise's great-grandad, who they were to collect from the care home in Valby, and Miss Martini from the first floor, but she'd had so much to drink that no one could understand anything she said, so she was staying home. But the party had gained another guest in the form of the second-hand dog. He was sitting in his cardboard box looking somewhat disgruntled, wearing two small devil horns which lit up red in the dark.

"Is this really necessary?" asked the dog.

Elise nodded.

"We're celebrating Halloween, so we need to be dressed up."

"Is that why there's a fat orange head on the window sill?"

"It's a pumpkin."

"Can't I just go as myself? A lot of people would say that's scary enough."

"Keep the horns on."

"You've not taken me out either, if you catch my drift."

"You'll have to hold it in. We're leaving in five minutes."

The dog sighed.

"As you will, lassie."

❖

Twenty minutes later, they were sitting in Aunt Fie's 2CV, which was such an antique it had cost twice the price of a new car, but it did ten kilometres on a cup of herbal tea, so it was paying for itself really. There wasn't much space, but everyone was in high spirits, and everyone was prepared for the worst. Fie had done something or other with one of her eyes so it looked like it was hanging halfway down her cheek, and Elise's dad, who was a Danish champion of misunderstanding, had put his clown costume on, so nothing was new there.

The roof of Fie's car could be rolled back, and when it was dry they usually did, giving Elise's dad room to play a folk melody on his violin.

It was a warm evening for the time of year, and there were a lot of children in the streets who waved at them as they made their way, with musical accompaniment, to Valby, where Elise's great-grandad lived. The care home was a big pink house, and outside the house there was a ghost – Great-Grandad – waving its stick at passers-by. This had nothing to do with it being Halloween – he always did that.

"What on earth is that thing?"

Elise said it was her dog.

"What's that smell?"

Elise said that if her dog smelled of anything, it was vermouth.

"Does it bite?"

"No, he doesn't bite," said Elise, "and if we hurry, he won't poop in the car either. I was so busy dressing up I didn't have time to take him out. Now I just hope he can hold it in."

Great-Grandad said he'd try to hold it in too.

❖

The trip up to Odsherred took about an hour, and they always sang two songs on the way: *Make Me Know Your Ways* and *Go Forth and Fish*.

Elise leaned back, closed her eyes and crossed

her fingers that her mum had received the parcel of salty liquorice. It was utterly impossible to find salty liquorice in Brazil, and salty liquorice was the only remedy for homesickness. That's why Elise had sent her mum a double portion, and as she sat there in the old 2CV, she imagined herself, her dog and her mum sitting on her suspension bridge munching on salty liquorice.

🐾

When they arrived, darkness had fallen around the windmill, which sat on the hill with a view of half of Odsherred and a bit of Isefjord.

Elise's grandma had hung a variety of rice-paper lanterns in the trees, and a yellow skull and crossbones over the door – the remains of a goat from a neighbouring farm.

There was a wonderful smell of rotting leaves and winter, and the deep-blue autumn sky above the windmill was so beautifully clear that Elise's dad said tonight you'd be able to see Saturn. Fie added that everything was written in the stars, and Great-Grandad said his toes were freezing.

Elise loved Halloween, and she loved her grandma, who always made the most of it, but most of all she loved her grandma's meatloaf, which they always ate on 31 October. However, before that they would have a glass of blood.

Grandma said she'd just drained the blood from three adorable children who'd come trick or treating.

"They sang together, each voice more lovely than the next, and when they were done, I invited them in and cut their throats with the breadknife."

"Serves them right," cackled Great-Grandad.

They drank the blood from tall, narrow glasses. It tasted just like tomato juice.

Elise's grandma was small and round, and it was her dearest ambition to become even rounder.

"Welcome," she said, "to the ghost house. I've been looking forward to your visit for a whole month. As you can see, my fingers are slightly dirty, and that's because I've been at the cemetery all day. I hope you're prepared for the worst. It will be interesting to see who this evening's next victim is."

"Me, I expect," said Great-Grandad. "I'm already half-dead."

❀

They kicked off the programme for the evening by sitting down to eat the meatloaf. After that Great-Grandad would give a speech – which would take some time since there was a lot he had to remember, and he didn't have the best memory – before all the lights were turned out and the real fun started. But before that, the adults would have a cognac, and Elise's dad would have a cigar, but not a real cigar, a joke cigar that went bang and made his face sooty. Then Grandma would have a glass of cognac for the other leg, and Great-Grandad would ask whether he could drink from the bottle, which he couldn't, but everyone knew he would as soon as the lights were turned off.

❀

Suffice to say, there were high expectations for the evening, and this was reflected in the night sky, which changed colour from deep blue to black. Out of pure curiosity, the stars gathered closer together, because it was on All Hallows' Eve you could see elves and fairies, witches from Bloksbjerg, and pixies flying around the church together like a swarm of fireflies.

But at midnight they would disappear, because that was when the real monsters came out.

7

The last day of October was coming to an end. Down by the elm trees the crows were cawing, but otherwise all was quiet.

They were seated around the windmill's beautiful table, which was lit by five tapers and six seven-armed candelabras.

The windmill had its own sound. Everything that lived in the nooks and crannies, and in the rafters – woodlice, earwigs, dormice and all the local spiders – was also celebrating All Hallows' Eve and throwing their own party, if the noise was anything to go by. The only thing you couldn't hear was the bats, who were hanging from the rafters, fast asleep.

Once they had eaten and toasted Countess Frandsen – whoever she was, but they always toasted

her – Grandma brandished her glass and announced that no one could leave the house from this point on.

"For tis the hour that the dead rise from their graves and make their way up to the mill. You can tell from the smell," she said.

"They should smell me," said Great-Grandad.

"As you already know," continued Grandma, "there are a million places to hide, some of which are occupied by guests from previous years. They don't look like much, but at midnight, when the wind picks up and the ancient millstones grind against each other, the vampires will wake from their slumber and go looking for warm throats."

Elise's dad wrung his clown hands.

"Are there really vampires?" he asked.

"There's at least one I know of," said Grandma, "and he'll do anything he can to drain every last drop of your blood."

"He'll not get anything from me," said Great-Grandad.

Grandma looked at her wine glass.

"I sense a strange atmosphere," she whispered, "but from this moment on it's every man for himself. The powers of darkness know you're here, but they'll find they're up against a family that won't go down without a fight. Let the hunt begin, and may the bravest of heart have the final word."

Elise glanced at her dad, who looked somewhat pale despite his clown make-up. He was usually the first to come a cropper. He loved Halloween, but had never particularly enjoyed witching hour. One year he'd even locked himself in the bathroom.

However, Elise had to leave the windmill briefly to take her dog out, and as she stood out in the deep darkness of Odsherred looking for Cassiopeia, her aunt appeared as well.

"Your dad's had his exploding cigar, and Grandma's sitting at the pump organ, so it's time I met the talking dog."

Elise told Fie her dog said the strangest things.

Fie kissed Elise on the cheek.

"You've always been a curious child, one who likes playing tricks on grown-ups. I could see it in you even when you were a baby, with your black hair sticking straight up. You were born with an ace up your sleeve, and now you've got a dog that can talk. What a trick, what a contrivance... bravo."

"Thanks," said Elise. "But my dog's neither a contrivance nor a trick. He speaks fluent Danish with a Scottish accent, and you should feel honoured we're letting you hear it."

Fie pressed her hands together in a show of deference.

"Oh, but I really am grateful, and as soon as Duddi says Peter Piper picked a peck of pickled peppers, I'll take you on an outing in the woods with a horse and cart, soap bubbles and the whole caboodle."

Elise said she looked forward to it.

Fie opened her coal-black devil's mouth and smiled. For someone's aunt she was very pretty, with unblemished skin, sparkling white teeth, green-blue cat eyes and a lot of platinum blonde hair, but this evening she looked scary, and Elise hoped she wouldn't stumble across the high-heeled devil when they were set loose in the dark mill. The idea was that everyone did all they could to scare the life out of the others, and Fie didn't pull her punches. However, she usually went after her big brother, Elise's dad, because he was – as Fie said – the weakest link, and she was only really satisfied once he'd fainted. The winner was the person who scared the others so much that they gave up, and last year Miss Martini had been awarded the trophy – a twenty-centimetre high zombie figurine – after she scared Great-Grandad so much that he had taken refuge at the bus stop down the road.

Fie sat down next to the second-hand dog.

"Hello there," she said. "I'm Anna Sophie van Helsing, also known as Aunt Fie, and normally I don't sit and talk to dogs – in fact, I feel quite foolish – but all the same here we are enjoying each other's company, so let's hear it, buster."

The second-hand dog turned his head towards Fie, one eye looking in one direction and the other another.

"That's quite the astigmatism," mumbled Fie.

"Woof," said the dog.

Fie turned to look at Elise.

"That sounded almost... dog-like."

Elise sat down next to her dog.

"McAduddi," she said, "tell Aunt Fie where you come from."

The second-hand dog reared up onto his back legs.

"Woof," he said. "Woof, woof."

"I'm told," said Fie, "that you come from Scotland? Is that true?"

"Woof," said the dog. "Woof."

"Or might it be that you and your bent legs have never set foot in Scotland?"

"Woof, woof, woof."

Fie smiled.

"This is fun. Can you say Gasværksvej?"

"Woof."

Fie got up.

"Nice try, Lissi, my girl. Duddi looks cute in his little light-up horns, and you can hardly smell the cheese."

Elise clenched her teeth.

"He can talk. He just doesn't want to."

Fie found her black lipstick and reapplied it.

"Sure. I don't expect he's in a reading mood either."

Elise gripped his collar.

"Why won't you say anything, you stupid dog?"

"Woof," said the dog.

Fie started heading back to the mill.

"See you in a bit, sweetie."

"Fie, wait!" shouted Elise, "Give him a chance!"

"Better luck next time."

Elise clenched her teeth and closed her eyes. A pump organ tune could be heard from up inside the mill, the only tune Grandma could play, an eerie mixture of *Lo, How a Rose E'er Blooming* and *Søren the Banjo Mouse*.

It was a beautiful evening. The new moon hung low over the blue fields in the night sky, and a narrow column of smoke rose from Rørvig.

Elise looked at the second-hand dog.

"I hope you realise you've made me look a fool. Fie was the only person I was going to let hear you talk, and you just sat there saying woof."

"Woof."

"Have you forgotten how to talk?"

"Woof."

Elise sighed.

"I'm going in now. You behave like a dog, and forget about getting the remains of the meatloaf for dinner. No talking, no meatloaf. Those are the rules, and you could do with losing a couple kilos anyway."

The second-hand dog went over to Elise.

"Careful now," he said. "No need to get personal. I'll be in shortly, I'm just going to do my business."

Elise put her hands on her hips, and even though she didn't want to, she started to giggle.

It looked like the dog was laughing too.

"Woof," he said. "I do enjoy a good woof... But jings, it's freezing out here in the sticks."

"It's not 'the sticks', and it's not even that cold."

"Maybe not," said the dog. "But then, you're not walking round with your bum out, are you?"

Elise smiled.

"I expect we can find a pair of long underwear for you if you like."

"Thanks," said the dog. "But I'd rather have a kilt. Say, do you know how the bagpipes were invented? Someone blew some air into a chicken, tied some string around its neck and pressed so hard on its belly that the air blew out of the other end, and then-"

"I'm going to stop you there," said Elise. "I don't need to hear your disgusting stories. We're here to have fun, and now Fie will never believe anything I say ever again. Thanks for that."

"I didn't mean to upset you," said the dog.

Elise sat down next to him.

"You didn't, not really, and actually I didn't know that was how the bagpipes were invented. Why is your breath so bad?"

The dog smiled.

"I ate a dead rodent and it seems it was a couple days past its sell-by date."

Elise rolled her eyes.

"Lovely. Here's some mints. They'll take the edge off."

The dog sighed.

"I'm sure you know man's a dog's best friend, right?"

"Yes, I know that, and you're my best friend. I really don't know what I'd do without you. It seems odd, looking at you."

The second-hand dog wagged his tail.

"Does that mean I get my ears scratched?"

Elise scratched behind the dog's ear.

"And the other one," he said.

Elise scratched behind the dog's other ear.

"And my back. Something's tickling me there. I think it might be a flea."

"OK," said Elise. "I'm going inside now."

The dog emptied the tin of mints.

"Hallelujah!" he shouted. "Sayonara, eau de dormouse! *Good evening, ladies and gentlemen. My name is McAduddi.*"

The second-hand dog jumped around on his back legs.

"It must be the mints. I'm on fire."

Elise headed for the mill.

"That's nice," she said. "But the evening's only just begun, so pace yourself."

♣

Elise, Aunt Fie, Elise's dad, Elise's grandma and Elise's great-grandad each had their own plan for the evening, but things rarely go as planned.

The ghost lurched down through the narrow hall and up the ladder leading from the ground floor to the first floor. From the way the ghost moved you could tell it was an elderly ghost, mostly because it walked with a stick.

Elise smiled. She'd never been afraid of ghosts, especially not ghosts with walking sticks, and in any case she was on her way down into the basement. There were no electric lights down there, so Elise had taken a candlestick with her, and she wasn't alone – she had the dog with her.

Elise had brought him up to speed.

"We're on a dangerous mission, so I'm glad to be the proud owner of a relentlessly vicious and aggressive guard dog."

The dog looked at her.

"Then why didn't we bring him?"

"I'm talking about you, blockhead. You need to look after me and listen out for even the faintest noise."

The dog said picking up faint noises wasn't really his strong suit since his hearing had never been that good. The only thing he always heard was something being decanted into his food bowl.

"Then you'll have to sniff them out," said Elise. "You can do that, right?"

The dog admitted he didn't have the best sense of smell either.

"You know what I think?" said Elise. "I think you're scared. I think we've forked out for a guard dog who's afraid of a game of hide and seek."

The dog said the whole "old windmill fancy dress" thing was a bit old hat.

"You think Halloween's old hat?"

The dog yawned.

"I've had worm treatments that were more fun."

Elise crossed her arms.

"So it's not just that you're a little crybaby who would pee his pants if he saw a ghost?"

"As you can see," said the dog, "I don't wear pants, so I couldn't pee my pants if I tried, and besides, I prefer being outside in the fresh air, snapping at earthworms."

"Snapping at earthworms?"

"They need snapping at, trust me."

Elise gripped his lead.

"You're coming with me."

🐾

It was pitch-dark in the basement, and what light the candlestick did provide only made the darkness more overwhelming. Elise stopped in the middle of the big room, sure she could hear something that sounded like breathing, something that wasn't her or the dog.

There was an old wardrobe standing against the wall. It had been used as a hiding place before. Elise remembered one year when her mum had stood in it with a rope around her neck. It had looked really scary, and Elise had vowed never to go into the basement

75

again and particularly not to open the wardrobe. Now she found herself in the basement despite herself, trying to convince herself she wasn't afraid.

She sat down next to the dog.

"In a moment," she whispered. "I'll open the old wardrobe and we'll deal with whatever's waiting in there."

The dog nodded.

"We could open the fridge too, and deal with whatever's in there."

"Yes, we could, but I want to win the trophy this year."

"And I want to nab the rest of the meatloaf. Those white bits were particularly good."

Elise sighed.

"Those white bits are lard. Fat – pig fat."

"And I thought they were particularly good."

Elise looked around.

"I know you're just a little second-hand dog with strange eating habits, but at least try to understand that a person needs to overcome their greatest fears.

I expect the same applies to dogs. What are you most scared of, Duddi?"

"I'm most scared of that bald guy filching the meatloaf."

"Are you talking about my great-grandad?"

"He's bald, isn't he?"

Elise took a deep breath and counted in a low, calm voice.

"When I open the wardrobe, it's to make sure there's nothing inside. That's how you face your fears. That's what brave girls and dogs do, and vampires aren't real, so you can... hey, have you got your eyes closed?"

"Not like we can see anything anyway."

"Stop that and open your eyes."

"Listen here," said the dog, "there's nothing wrong with family gatherings, but if you want to have a nice time, why didn't we go to McDonald's? You should see me demolish a burger. Big Mac, Quarter Pounder, McFeast, Cheeseburger, Hamburger, McChicken, large fries, small fries..."

"Yeah, alright, I get it."

"You can get sauce for the fries too. I could eat that by the shovelful. Me and my brothers lived behind McDonald's in Tobermory for three years, and we never went to bed hungry. Eventually we got so fat we needed help to scratch behind our ears."

"Well, congratulations, but we're not at McDonald's now, we're at my grandma's windmill."

Elise took a deep breath, counted to three and opened the wardrobe.

It was empty apart from a pile of clothes in the bottom.

"Thank goodness," said Elise. "I was sure there was someone in here."

Then she noticed three fingers sticking out from behind the pile of clothes.

Elise stiffened, sure that the dog had also seen them before attaching himself to her leg.

Elise grabbed the clothes and pulled them away.

Her dad was sitting in the bottom of the wardrobe. He was quite a tall man, but he looked small in the empty space.

"Oh, thank heavens," he whimpered. "It's only you, Elise."

Elise moved the candle closer to his face.

"You're white as a sheet."

He gestured to his costume.

"I don't know whether you've noticed, but I'm dressed like a clown, and clowns do tend to have white faces."

Elise's dad looked around before pulling Elise down to his level.

"But never mind that. Something's very, very wrong."

"How do you mean?"

"I mean something doesn't add up."

Elise sat down on the edge of the wardrobe floor.

"You shut yourself in a wardrobe because something doesn't add up?"

Her dad chewed nervously at his knuckle.

"I went up to the attic to find Great-Grandad so we could execute our plan."

"You had a plan? How organised."

Elise's dad grabbed hold of her and lowered his voice.

"We were going to get one over on Fie this year. She thinks she can scare the life out of all of us, so this year your great-grandad and I agreed we'd pip her to the post."

"How?"

"Your great-grandad was going to sit on my shoulders to make a ghost that was three metres tall. I actually had him up on my shoulders – and believe me, it's not easy to keep your balance when you're wearing size 55 clown shoes – and when we left the attic we could see your grandma in the vegetable garden out the window, which meant we just had to find Fie, so we went downstairs, with your great-grandad still on my shoulders – which wasn't easy, but I only dropped him once – and then I spotted Fie in the dining room, and that's when it happened."

"What?" said Elise.

"Something came through the wall."

Elise tilted her head quizzically.

"Dad, be reasonable. Something came through

the wall? Grandma was in the garden, Fie was in the dining room, and I was outside. How could anything have come through the wall?"

Elise's dad sighed.

"That's what I'm saying – something doesn't add up! That's one too many people. Unless, Elise... unless it was a vampire."

"Oh, for heaven's sake. A vampire? Haven't you always told me there's no such thing? Isn't that what you've been telling me my entire life?"

Her dad took his clown nose off.

"Can we forget about that for now? Now, you and your dog go upstairs and find out what's going on. I'll stay here and hold the fort."

Elise asked him what the ghost had looked like.

He put his nose back on.

"It was pale, almost transparent, with two glowing red eyes, and unless I'm much mistaken, two very long, sharp fangs."

The corners of his clown mouth turned down.

"I just want to be at home with the weeping fig."

Elise put a hand on her dad's shoulder.

"But you're not at home, Dad, you're sitting in a wardrobe in Odsherred. Don't worry though, my guard dog and I will go upstairs and sort all this out."

Elise's dad took her hand.

"You've always been so brave. Remember that time you fell and needed stitches at the hospital? Five stitches in your arm. It was horrible, but you were so brave."

Elise nodded.

"You were brave too once they'd given you something to calm you down."

Her dad sighed.

"Elise, I hope you know I'm proud of you. Though I'm happier knowing you'll have your dog with you."

Elise looked at the dog, who was still plastered to her leg.

"Yeah," she said. "He's a savage beast, this one."

Five minutes later, Elise and the dog were standing on the mill's snow-covered front steps.

Elise checked the dog knew what their mission was.

The dog said they were outside to stretch their legs.

"And I need to pee."

"You just went."

"I didn't get to finish, and it's very important to let a dog finish peeing. Besides, I'm no hunter. If you wanted a hunting dog, you should have got a golden retriever."

Elise loomed over the dog.

"Would you really let me down now?"

"I do actually need to pee. My bladder's so full I slosh when I walk."

Elise put a hand on the dog's back.

"I asked you a question. Would you really let me down now?"

The dog shook his head.

"No," he groaned. "Of course not. It would take more than that for me to let a friend down... cocktail sausages, for instance."

"Good, then let's make a move. I'll make myself look as big as possible, and you bare your teeth."

"All five of them?"

"All five of them. Let's go."

9

All was quiet inside the mill. The only sound was the creaking of the crooked stairs, which gave slightly when someone trod on them.

Elise opened a small, round window. The view of the starry sky was nothing short of spectacular. Everything was as expected: the light over Isefjord, the crows in the elm trees and the icy blue half-moon. But one thing couldn't be explained.

Elise sighed. There didn't have to be an explanation for everything. It was nice that some things still couldn't be explained, that people couldn't – as Miss Martini put it – reduce life down into facts and figures. But spectres and ghosts needed thorough investigation, preferably with a magnifying glass. Elise didn't have a magnifying glass, so she would

have to make do with her senses, and they were on high alert.

She crept along on her tiptoes until she was standing in front of the door to Grandma's bedroom. Maybe the ghost was in there. The light was on in any case and – Elise thought – it was strangely quiet.

She looked at her dog.

"Ready?" she asked.

"The batteries are dead," said the dog.

"What batteries?"

"The batteries for my devil horns. I hate these horns."

Elise bent down towards the dog.

"Well, excuse me, but it was an attempt to make you look just a bit scarier."

"I suppose," said the dog. "But they're out of juice. Can I take them off? There's no such thing as a dog with antlers, as far as I know."

Elise bent down towards the dog again.

"You'll keep them on. Now let's puff out our chests and go in."

"I can't puff my chest out like that. I have asthma."

"Honestly, how pathetic can you get?"

"You don't know what it's like. You walk around breathing like it's the most natural thing in the world while poor orphan dogs with bad hips like me fight for every breath. The air in this museum piece doesn't make it any better, plus it's been ages since I was thoroughly groomed."

"You what?"

"When you have a dog, it's important that you check your dog's fur once a week, and there's something wrong with my belly – scabies or mould, I don't know which."

"See what I'm doing?"

"What are you doing?"

"Opening the door."

🐾

Grandma was sitting on the bed. She had taken her wig off.

"Oh, Elise," she said. "Hello there, sweetheart."

Elise looked around.

"Why are you sitting in here? Why aren't you out there trying to scare the others?"

Grandma invited Elise to sit with her on the bed.

"I have something to tell you, but you have to promise you won't tell anyone. I ran into your aunt down in the kitchen."

"In the kitchen?"

"Yes, she was sitting between the wine racks."

"What was she doing there?"

"She was shaking."

"Aunt Fie? No way."

Grandma crossed herself and knocked on the wooden table.

"She was in the blue corridor sneaking up on your great-grandad, not that he can hear or see, especially not with a bed sheet over his head – which reminds me, we need to get someone to look at the lump on his forehead."

Elise crossed her arms.

"What happened up there?"

Grandma took a deep breath.

"At first Fie thought she'd seen your dad, but your dad had gone down into the basement, you were standing on the path up to the door with your dog and I was in the vegetable garden. You see? We're not alone."

"I know," said Elise. "I just talked to Dad and he said the same thing."

Grandma pulled Elise towards her.

"There's a bond between us," she whispered. "A strong bond. You and I don't cower in fear when life challenges us. All our family is the same, the women, at least – your dad bails at the drop of a hat and your great-grandad's so out of it he ended his speech at dinner by wishing us all a happy Easter." Grandma sighed. "And now that Fie's thrown in the towel, it's only you left."

Elise shot her Grandma a sideways glance.

"What do you mean it's only me left?"

Grandma shrugged, suddenly looking very tired.

"Only you left in the daily struggle to keep our heads held high, to be happy, not miserable and out of sorts. It's easy to let the gloom drag you down during the autumn. But you've always been our guiding light. I'll never forget when you were Lucia. It was just magical until your hair caught fire."

Elise let herself flop back onto the bed.

"Sometimes it's hard to be brave," she mumbled.

Grandma nodded.

"But we mustn't give up," she whispered. "Halloween is special. I look forward to it all year. Why? Because it's when I can dress up and play the fool, but deep down I'm still just me. Maybe I need to put a mask on every once in a while. I was thinking about it while setting the table. No doubt you noticed I set one too many places?"

Elise nodded.

Grandma nodded as well before closing her eyes.

"When I feed the birds in the morning, I say the most terrible things."

"I don't expect they mind. Besides, it's good to let it all out."

"I couldn't hold it in, that's for sure."

"What are you saying?"

Grandma sighed.

"I'm saying to hell with that bridge."

Elise sat up and put her arms around her grandma.

"But people need it."

"And to hell with the people. Let them row! They've got boats, right?"

Then Grandma sighed again.

"I suppose you're right," she said. "It'll be good for them to have that bridge, and I'm very proud of her, knowing she can build such a thing. I can't even repair the stepladder and I've never travelled further than Karlsruhe... but why couldn't she be building a bridge over Isefjord? Why does she have to be on the other side of the world?"

Grandma walked over to a small display cabinet and took out a bottle of red liquid.

"It's got St John's wort in it. It's good for colds, loneliness and sorrow."

Grandma poured herself a dram and downed it in one.

"Did it help?" asked Elise.

Grandma poured some more.

"Not in the slightest."

"You should try salty liquorice."

Grandma buried her face in her hands, and for a moment it sounded like she was crying, but she wasn't, she was laughing.

Elise laughed too, though she wasn't sure why.

Grandma sighed.

"Life isn't for wimps, and I have so much to be thankful for – my lovely family, my halfway decent health and my hobbies. I do flower arranging, potato-printing and rhythmic gymnastics."

"Is gymnastics fun?"

"It's boring and makes my neck cramp, but what can I do? Are you ever lonely, Elise? No doubt children get lonely sometimes too."

Elise shrugged.

"Yes, I think they do, but I have my dog."

Grandma nodded.

"And I have my windmill and my stiff-legged

gymnastics friends, not to mention my St John's wort snaps. I suppose we shouldn't complain, but nine months is a long time, and yesterday evening I sat looking at her confirmation picture for so long I swear it started to fade. Have you seen your mum's confirmation picture? She had braces back then. Oh, how she hated having her picture taken! She's never seemed older than fourteen to me."

Grandma put her hand on Elise's cheek.

"And since it's Halloween, I don't think it's untoward to say you look scarily like her, especially with that axe in your forehead. Anyway, let's get back to it. All good to go, sweetie?"

Sweetie was.

Grandma opened a drawer in her bureau and took out a bottle of green liquid and a crucifix, which she set down in front of Elise. Elise asked what they were for.

Grandma winked at her.

"This bottle contains a decilitre of holy water from Matas, and I got the crucifix at a flea market in Højby.

They're the only things that will help."

"With what?"

"Vampires."

Elise looked at her dog, who seemed to be having trouble breathing and was sitting with his tongue hanging out of his mouth.

Grandma lit a cigar and gave it such a good puff that she disappeared into a cloud of grey smoke for a moment. Elise said she thought Grandma had stopped smoking. Grandma said she stopped smoking three times a week.

"My darling girl, do an old woman a favour and

take that crucifix. Then he won't be able to hurt you if you come across him."

"Grandma, I don't believe in vampires."

"I understand, but you don't know the story of Putte Svendsen, the miller."

"What about him?"

"Svendsen was the first miller on the land register, back in eighteen-somethingorother, and they say he's buried under the mill in a black iron coffin, which is fine in and of itself, but people in the area claim Svendsen didn't die of natural causes. Indeed, some people even say he didn't die at all, and that he turns up in the winter out on the streets, baring his terrible teeth. He tried to get into the church during the harvest thanksgiving service, but the schoolmaster's wife stopped him. Svendsen's very active at this time of year, and a week ago they found three dead sheep behind the supermarket in Vig."

Elise nodded.

"And people think Putte Svendsen had something to do with it?"

Grandma sighed.

"So they say, and there's more superstition and witchcraft out in the countryside than in the cities. That was actually why I moved here. But now, you take that old crucifix, just like your old grandma says. And here, take this mirror too."

"What's that for?"

Grandma squeezed Elise's hand.

"Vampires don't have reflections."

Elise put her hands on her hips.

"Alright, that's enough, I think I'll leave all this with you. I have something ten times better – my dog."

Elise had barely managed to finish her sentence before the dog started coughing uncontrollably.

Elise told Grandma about the asthma.

"And anyway, I don't believe in vampires, and neither does my guard dog. I admit I'm a bit confused by what you've told me, but it doesn't scare me, it just makes me even more determined, and now Duddi and I are going upstairs to find out what's going on. Good day to you."

10

And so Elise and her guard dog made their way up the narrow spiral staircase, round and round. Outside the wind tore at the blades of the windmill, and down below they could hear the heavy millstones grinding against each other like in days gone by.

The second-hand dog stared at Elise.

"What was all that about Putte Svendsen?"

"Nothing."

"The man killed three sheep."

"Duddi, you shouldn't believe everything my grandma says. At Midsummer she said the mayor had been out flying around on a neon tube like it was a broomstick."

"What, so the old mare's a couple sandwiches short of a picnic?"

Elise gave the dog a tight smile.

"It's nothing you need to worry about, and my grandma isn't actually that old, and let me tell you-"

Elise stopped talking and pressed herself up against the wall. She couldn't believe her eyes. There was a mummy standing five metres from them. It was, as mummies generally are, wrapped in long white bandages which covered its entire body, including its head.

Elise crouched down next to the second-hand dog.

"Do you see what I see?" she whispered.

"Yeah," said the dog. "A kitchen roll with legs."

Elise shook her head.

"It's a mummy," she snapped. "A dead person walking."

"Sooo... time to run?"

Elise grabbed the dog as the mummy staggered towards them on wobbly legs. A hoarse sound came from its mouth.

Elise stood up straight.

"You can't scare me," she whispered.

"And I can't breathe," gasped the mummy.

Elise squinted.

"Great-Grandad?"

"Well, I sure as hell ain't Tutankhamun. Get me out of this."

Elise grabbed one of the bandages and started to pull. Great-Grandad span round and round until he was free.

"Urgh, now I'm dizzy," he groaned. "But what else is new? I love being old, but I hate Easter."

Elise put her hand on Great-Grandad's shoulder.

"That's quite a lump you've got on your forehead."

"It's bigger than an ostrich egg," moaned Great-Grandad. "And I broke four vertebrae when I fell off your dad's shoulders. At least my hearing seems to have improved. Now I'm going to have a double brandy, but just so you Halloween halfwits know, I'm still a mummy. Ain't no breathing any life into me."

❧

Shortly afterwards, Elise and the second-hand dog found themselves in the blue corridor with its old portraits of former millers. Just by looking at their white faces, you would be forgiven for thinking they might come back to haunt the place. One in particular was very pale. Perhaps he was Svendsen. Either way, his pallor was less than healthy, and those were some very pointy teeth.

"But really, the only reason they're so white is because of all the flour in the mill back then," whispered Elise.

"Correction," said the dog, "They're white because their blood's been drained. Putte Svendsen has risen again. He will come for us, and we'll end up as vampires doomed to roam the wilds of Holbæk for evermore."

"Get a grip. It's Halloween and we're here to have fun."

"I can see it in your eyes, lassie, everything's gone wrong. We dogs have a sixth sense, and I can feel something's not right. I can feel it in my gut."

"Ew."

Elise looked around.

It was quiet and very dark up on the top floor of the mill. What little light there was came from a small skylight, which let dusty moonbeams fall onto the bare wooden floorboards.

Elise sat down next to the dog.

"There's no reason to blow things out of proportion, and anyway, there's nothing wrong with being a little bit scared. It's actually very human, even for a dog. Not that there's anything to be scared of."

The dog closed his eyes.

"Stop kidding yourself, love. There's someone here."

"It's just us," whispered Elise.

"And the ghost. It's behind the grandfather clock. Here's hoping it isn't Putte Svendsen."

Elise clenched her teeth.

"If you say Putte Svendsen one more time, I swear to God."

"I don't want to end up like those dead sheep behind the supermarket."

"Then zip it."

Elise looked around, only now spotting the narrow grandfather clock against the wall. It hadn't worked for years. It was said the clock was as old as the mill, and that it only chimed once a year, at midnight on New Year's Eve. But the mill – not to mention Elise's grandma – was full of such stories.

Elise smiled.

"Aw, is the little doggy scared of the grandfather clock?"

"No, I'm scared of what's hiding behind it. So that's me away. I need to go to Odsherred. Perhaps I'll find a ladybird to arm wrestle. See you around, lassie."

"You're staying here."

"Can you really not hear it?"

Elise closed her eyes.

"Hear what? I don't hear anything."

Elise took two steps forward so she was standing a few centimetres away from the brown face of the grandfather clock. Oddly enough, it sounded like the clock was working, and even though the ticking noise was innocent enough, it gave Elise goosebumps.

"I thought it only worked on New Year's Eve," she whispered.

Suddenly there was a faint scratching noise. Then the clock chimed three times.

Elise's mouth went dry. The second-hand dog threw himself down on his stomach with his paws over his ears.

Elise stayed upright, turning to gawp at the figure coming out from behind the clock. It was hard to tell whether it was a man or a woman, but whatever it was, it had a pale, almost bloodless face with two deep-set red eyes. But what stood out most was its teeth, which were long and yellow, like fangs.

"What did I tell you?" moaned the dog. "It's Putte Svendsen come to put an end to our fun."

"I'm not so sure about that," Elise whispered, watching the vampire with a small smile.

There might not have been a lot of light in the corridor, but the smell of Martini was unmistakeable.

"Are you the vampire everyone's scared of?"

"I'm Prutte Svansen," babbled the vampire.

Elise put her hands on her hips and looked up at the ceiling.

"Don't you mean Putte Svendsen?"

"Yes," said the vampire. "Putte Svansen."

"I'm Elise from Mysundegade," said Elise.

"And I'm out of here," said the dog.

"Look out," burbled the ghost. "Look out for the man with the fings, fongs... sharp wotsits."

"Fangs?" said Elise, smiling.

"That's the ones!" mumbled the vampire, bumping into the wall.

"Alright," said Elise. "Party's over. Time to take the teeth out, Miss Martinsen."

It was suddenly very quiet.

"Botheration!" said a very familiar voice.

Miss Martini took the vampire fangs out of her mouth and gave Elise a quick hug.

"I have to admit," said Miss Martini, "it all sounded foolproof when we arranged it on... the wotsit, you know, the... er?"

"On the phone?" suggested Elise.

"Right, on the phone. Your dad didn't know anything about it, he'd never have had any part in tricking you. It was all your rubbish...er...wait... AUNT'S idea. She's so resourceful, and she means well, you know. I myself donate money to a charity for cats. What were we talking about? Ah yes, it's actually not all that fun being a vampire, and I didn't get any meatloaf or gherkins. And I really like gherkins."

Elise put her arm around the elderly lady.

"But the vampire was a good idea," she said. "And the thing with the clock was really cool, the way you made it chime three times."

Miss Martini's eyes widened.

"It made all my hair stand on end."

Elise looked around.

"That was you, right?"

Miss Martini said she hadn't touched the old clock.

"Well," said Elise. "Let's head down, shall we? Quickly now. Come on."

🐾

October gave way to November, Halloween drew to a close, and the trophy was awarded to Great-Grandad for what must have been some laborious work with twenty rolls of bandages. Grandma stood in front of the mill and waved goodbye with two sparklers as the old 2CV rolled away down the hill.

Since Elise's dad was playing Albinoni, Great-Grandad was snoring and Miss Martini was babbling away in Chinese, the second-hand dog felt he should contribute something too, so he started to howl at the moon, but when that was cut short by his asthma, he made do with coughing.

11

November days are veiled by drizzle, and one hazy Thursday a small fairy meandered its way down Strøget, Copenhagen's main shopping street. The fairy was wearing a pink skirt, a pair of blue wellies and an IKEA hat. Apart from that she was dressed warmly against the Siberian wind.

Elise – because of course it was her – had put the dog in her rucksack so she could carry a mug of hot soup in each hand. She was the November soup fairy, and now she had collected the soup from Fiolstraede behind the cathedral, she was on her way back to Illum department store, where he dad was playing his violin.

There were a lot of people on the street, but if the contents of her dad's violin case were anything to go by, people were either really preoccupied by their Christmas shopping or really couldn't stand Albinoni. Either way, it was woefully empty.

Her dad, who was wearing his Santa outfit, had been standing on the street for six hours, so he was very pleased to see the soup fairy.

"Though I'm afraid my violin case is far from overflowing," he said, blowing on the soup.

Elise sat on a bike rail.

"Maybe you should play something other than Albinoni."

Her dad said he always played Albinoni in November, but it didn't help that the hairs of his violin bow had become so frayed he needed to go and get a new one. Otherwise Albinoni would never forgive him.

Elise looked at her dad.

"I thought he was dead."

"Well, I'm afraid he is, dead and buried, but he looks down from heaven every time someone plays his music. That's why you have to make an effort."

Elise smiled.

"Do you think Albinoni would like it more if you got a new bow?"

Her dad said he was sure of it, but there weren't many music shops that sold second-hand bows.

"But we could cycle out to see Kalle Krudtkarl in Palermovej, he usually has one or two in his back room."

Elise liked going to Kalle Krudtkarl's. He was a clever man with an African wife who made sweets for the customers. The last time Elise had been there, she had learned how difficult it was to play the tuba with a mouthful of caramel.

Her dad went to fetch his cargo bike, which was locked to a lamppost in Silkegade.

While he was doing that, Elise looked in on the dog.

"We're going to Amager," she said.

"I'll stay here and hold down the fort," said the dog.

"There's no need," said Elise. "And you'll like the trip across the bridge. You may have noticed our family has something of a bridge fixation."

The dog shook his head.

"I'll get travel sick on that thing. My stomach will start gurgling, and then, all of a sudden, I'll be able to taste the liver pâté I ate last summer."

Elise rolled her eyes.

"OK, but don't go anywhere. Stay in front of Illum."

The dog jumped out of her rucksack.

"Where would I go? I'll look after the three bottle caps your dad's earned. Maybe I'll get up on my hind legs and dance a bit, people love seeing an overweight dog dance. I can walk on my hands too."

"You don't have hands."

"Why do you always have to burst my bubble?"

Elise sat down next to the dog.

"Promise you won't run away?"

"Would you miss me?"

"Maybe."

"Wormed my way into your heart, have I, lassie?"

Elise crossed her arms.

"Do you really think anyone could be that nuts about a fat little dog who smells of cheese? You can't even give me your paw."

"No, but I can stick my tongue out. Want to see the red carpet?"

"Nah, you're alright."

"Lassie, there's something I wanted to ask you about. I was wondering if I could get one of those bones people use to make soup."

"Those bones aren't free."

"I know that," said the dog. "But if everyone pitches in and the moolah's to be had…"

"Moolah?"

"Yes, the money. You know, that green stuff your dad can't seem to make, and after hearing him play that fiddle, I'm not sure we should expect a Christmas miracle."

Elise put her forehead against the dog's.

"You have no appreciation for music. My dad has played in symphony orchestras, a string trio – he's even played timpani."

"In front of Illum?"

"Not in front of Illum, you dolt. In Næstved."

Elise looked at her dad, who was wheeling his bike towards them. His skin had that blue tinge it always got when he'd been standing in the cold for too long.

Elise said goodbye to the dog, who sat down next to the violin case containing eighteen kroner and three beer bottle caps.

❧

Ten minutes later, Elise and her dad were riding over Knippel Bridge, which was 115 metres long. Elise knew all there was to know about the bridges in Denmark. Her favourite was Toldbro Bridge in Ribe, which was more than a hundred years old. Exactly two years ago she had been sitting in Ribe eating red sausages with her mum. Her mum's love of red sausages was almost as great as her love of bridges. But now they were going to Amager, Elise's dad pumping the pedals hard to keep warm. He said if he could get a bow for a decent price, he would cycle back to Strøget and keep playing until Illum closed. People were extra generous at closing time, and that meant rice pudding for dessert.

Whenever they cycled out to see Kalle Krudtkarl in Amager, Elise's dad would sing a song he had written himself, and since Elise had heard it so many times, she always sang along.

> *Kalle from Palermovej*
> *His wife can hold a tune*
> *She comes from far-off Zanzibar*
> *And plays the bassoon.*

> *Kalle from Palermovej*
> *His wife she is so sweet*
> *You'll find her at Bo-bi Bar*
> *Her playing's just a treat.*

> *Kalle from Palermovej*
> *His wife she is just swell*
> *She can play most anything*
> *The gramophone as well.*

Elise's dad was very good at imitating musical instruments, particularly the bassoon, but truth be told, Kalle Krudtkarl's wife didn't play anything but the odds on pigeon races.

An hour later, her dad had obtained a violin bow that was as good as new, and Elise had been given some toffee that tasted so good she decided to save some for later in the evening, though she was also crossing her fingers for rice pudding all the way back from Amager, and perhaps it worked, because when they reached Illum, there were several hundred kroner in the violin case.

Elise's dad's jaw dropped.

"Well, I'll be. Perhaps the soup fairy crossing her fingers did help."

"I prayed to God as well," said Elise.

"And to Mr Mortensen?" said her dad.

Elise nodded. She had also prayed to Mr Mortensen. The first time Elise had heard about Mr Mortensen was when Miss Martini was going to the hospital to have her appendix removed. Elise had been standing in the street with her dad when the ambulance came to collect the old lady.

"We'll pray to God that it all goes well," Elise had said.

"Yes," said Miss Martini. "And if God's not home, pray to Mr Mortensen."

Since then Elise had always prayed to both God and Mr Mortensen.

But on this evening in the bluish darkness of November she did not think that God or Mr Mortensen had anything to do with suddenly having the money to buy rice pudding, and when they were cycling home to Mysundegade and Elise was sitting in the cargo bike with the second-hand dog in her lap, she asked him whether he knew where the money had come from.

"It came as if heaven sent," said the dog.

Elise smiled.

"And you didn't have a paw in it?"

The dog yawned.

"I may have had a wee dance," he said. "And what

can I say? I'm a great dancer."

Elise smiled.

"Clearly people liked it."

The dog sighed.

"It's not every day you see an overweight mongrel dancing the mazurka on Strøget, so when you go into town to buy me a bone tomorrow, make sure it's a big one. You know what I mean, a proper thigh bone to fill the hole that'll be left in my stomach after this death trap makes me puke. Hear it rumbling? Yikes, that's not good. Let's hope it's just a wee fart."

Elise shook her head.

"You're really gross."

"I know," said the dog. "I know, lassie."

☙

Three hours later, Elise was lying under her duvet and the dog was lying in his cardboard box next to the bed. Elise and her dad had looked at the stars, Elise had eaten the toffee from Palermovej, and now her dad had gone to watch the second half of Liverpool versus Sunderland.

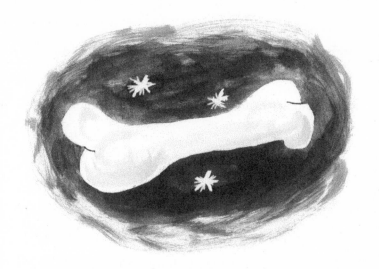

The second-hand dog gave Elise a sly look.

"Do you know Pluto's secret?"

"It has a secret?"

"If you point your telescope at Pluto, you can see your heart's desire."

"My telescope isn't good for anything."

"I don't have a telescope at all," said the dog. "But I see my heart's desire when I look at Pluto."

Elise lifted the second-hand dog up into her bed.

"So what do you see when you look at Pluto?"

The dog licked his lips.

"I see the butcher's biggest bone. I think it's a

thigh bone from a big, strapping cow. You could gnaw on a bone like that for days. Cows are my favourite animals, apart from salted herring. Can I come under the duvet?"

"Dad would rather you slept in the box. We haven't got rid of your fleas yet."

"I don't sleep well at all in that cardboard box. You know why? Because I'm not a tin of plum tomatoes."

"OK, OK, you can stay up here, you little pest."

The dog asked Elise about her heart's desire.

Elise thought about it for a while before pointing at the drawing of the yellow plane with the Brazilian flag on it.

"That's my mum's plane," she said. "But what about your mum, Duddi?"

"My mum?"

"I assume you have one."

The dog sighed.

"All dogs have mums, even dogs without collars."

"Where's your mum now?"

"Where's my mum? She went to Aberdeen."

Elise nodded.

"I thought as much. Don't you miss her?"

The dog smiled.

"I was the harbour's ugliest stray, but I always walked with my tail held high. I was the pride of Tobermory!"

"So you never miss her?"

"Never. Or very rarely, anyway. That's to say, sometimes. Usually in the evening."

"What do you do when you miss her?"

"I walk around with my tail between my legs. ... why are we talking about this?"

Elise shook her head.

"We don't have to, it's just all this talk of heart's desires."

For a moment it was very quiet in the flat.

"Are you sad because your mum's away, lassie?"

Elise said she wasn't.

The dog tilted his head sceptically.

"You look it. You are allowed to be sad, you know, it happens to the best of us, especially when we're trying to sleep. I expect you sometimes climbed into bed with your mum."

Elise stared into space. She had almost forgotten what it was like to lie down next to her mum. Her mum always had the same smell, the smell of soapflakes, toothpaste, rain and tobacco smoke. It was a big secret that Elise's mum snuck out onto the kitchen stairs to smoke a cigarette after dinner. As far as Elise knew, there were no kitchen stairs in the rainforest, but her mum would probably find somewhere to smoke all the same. It was difficult to imagine what her mum might smell like when she came home. Maybe she would just smell like suspension bridge. Maybe she would never smell the same again.

Elise looked up at the big, brown blotches on the ceiling. They were often the last thing she saw before she fell asleep. She had always imagined those blotches to be a map with mountains, rivers, cities and forests. Huge rainforests with dangerous animals and big suspension bridges.

"Something wrong, lassie?" asked the dog, and Elise said nothing was wrong.

"I'm sure I could think of something funny to say if that would help. I know a joke about a cat and a canary."

"Do you know what I have under my pillow, Duddi?"

"Cocktail sausages?"

Elise shook her head.

"Letters."

"Letters?"

Elise nodded.

"They're taped together because I tore them up when I got them. I threw one of them out the window and had to go out and collect all the pieces. I didn't lose a lot of it, just a few small words. The wind must have taken them, and I think lots of love must still be dancing around on the breeze. The same thing happened when I tried to answer the letters. I spent so long writing to her, my mum I mean, that it ended the same way, because when the letter was finished, I ripped it to shreds and sent the whole thing to Brazil as a jigsaw puzzle."

Elise looked at her dog.

"When you lived in Scotland, Duddi, where did you sleep? Did you have somewhere nice to stay?"

The second-hand dog snuggled down under the warm duvet.

"In Scotland I slept on ten eiderdown pillows, I had three poodles to serve me and a silk mouse to play with. There were meatballs, cocktail sausages and bones to chew on morning, noon and night. It has to be said, those really were the days."

Elise kissed the dog on the forehead and switched off the bedside lamp.

For a long time it was quiet in the room, then the dog asked whether Elise sometimes walked around with her tail between her legs too, and Elise said that if she had a tail, it would probably have hung between her legs every now and then.

Elise put her hand on the dog's head.

"You and I, McAduddi, are actually more alike than

we think, and you know what they say: two heads are better than one."

"Yes," said the dog. "That's almost twice as many."

"And you can count too."

"Ask me whatever you like and I'll work it out."

"OK, what's forty-seven plus nineteen?"

"Are we talking about tomatoes or bones?"

Elise smiled.

"Does it matter?"

The dog rolled onto his side.

"Dearie me, of course it matters! *Does it matter*, I ask you. You've got a lot to learn. Sleep well, my wee lassie."

"Same to you, my wee Duddi."

12

Aunt Fie had given Elise a gift calendar. It contained a small present for every day in December, and on this clear and frosty morning the present was wrapped in a page from a Lithuanian newspaper. All of Fie's presents were something she had found in the street or something she had scavenged from somewhere. It might be a box that she had painted, a poster made of tax receipts or, like today, half a chestnut and five elastic bands made into a ring.

Elise was like Fie in that she also loved things she had found herself, and in April, when she had been at the baker's buying morning rolls, she found a stone with a hole in it, which combined with a red shoelace became a piece of jewellery that she sent straight to Brazil.

But today was different. Elise had a somewhat specific plan for this Saturday, which started with her finding her old money box, which contained five baby teeth, a porcelain elephant from Lyø and all of her savings. She had earned most of it going into town for Miss Martini, but in the last couple of weeks she had earned a bit extra by cleaning Potifar's pet shop, and now she had eighty kroner, and that was really good considering how much she had spent on salty liquorice.

When Potifar asked what she would spend her savings on and Elise said it was for Christmas presents, the odd man had given Elise a bag of spices for Aunt Fie and an Egyptian drinking straw for Miss Martini. That was when Elise had invited Potifar and his wife over for Christmas Eve, which delighted Potifar since he and his wife usually celebrated Christmas by walking up to Frederiksberg Town Hall, where they would stand with their sparklers and listen to the bells.

♣

Now Elise only needed a present for her grandma, her great-grandad and her dad, but Grandma didn't like receiving Christmas presents, so she just got an extra hug, whereas Great-Grandad was becoming more and more demanding; last year he had cut out a photo of Miss Mexico and asked whether he could have her as his new home help.

Finally, there was the patient checkout lady from Netto, or as Elise's dad called her, the angel from Ulaanbaatar. A few years ago she had found out that the checkout lady's family were ten thousand miles away in a mountain village and that the checkout lady would spend Christmas with her budgie, but Elise's dad hadn't been able to cope with that notion, so now the checkout lady and her budgie always came to theirs on Christmas Eve, and it was just as well, because the checkout lady was the only person who could make gravy, and when they asked her what she wanted for Christmas, she always said she wanted to take the leftovers from their Christmas dinner home with her, and you might think that was a reasonable request, but Great-Grandad always wanted to take the leftovers home too, and he thought the Grauballe Man from Valby was more entitled to the last duck leg than the checkout lady from Mongolia, so that was why Elise's dad always – shortly before dinner – made up two identical doggy bags, one for Great-Grandad and one for the angel from Ulaanbaatar.

That left Elise's dad, who never wanted anything even though he didn't have much. This year, even though he only wore a tie when he played at funerals, Elise had decided that she would buy – not a tie, that was too boring – a chequered bow tie from the nice shop on Vesterbrogade that sold clothes for important businessmen. Unfortunately the bow tie cost three hundred kroner, and even though Elise had been in to ask whether they'd consider selling it for fifty kroner and a baby tooth, they were not swayed – the green chequered bow tie cost three hundred kroner, with or without teeth.

"Why not make a bow tie using your own fair sausage fingers?" asked the second-hand dog.

"Because I don't have enough material," said Elise. "Besides, you can't just make a bow tie from an old pair of grey woolly socks."

"Does it have to have green checks?"

Elise said it could have yellow checks, but it had to be chequered, because that was the height of fashion among businessmen, and to that the dog said all they needed to do was nip down to Gasværksvej, to the pizzeria that sold the best pizza Margherita with all the trimmings in the whole city.

Elise shook her head.

"We're talking about my dad's Christmas present, and all you can think about is stuffing your face."

"Lassie," said the dog. "Close your eyes and imagine I'm your guide dog."

"I don't want to be blind."

"Imagine I'm the dog who guides your every step and gets you safely across roads and down to McDonald's, where we don't go often – more's the pity – but in any case, imagine you trust my senses entirely."

Elise closed her eyes.

"So?"

"So you would follow me to the ends of the earth, even for your dad's Christmas present."

❧

Papa Giorgio's Best Pizza Bar – eat in or take away was a highly frequented pizzeria on Gasværksvej.

Elise and the second-hand dog had trudged down Istedgade and were now standing outside.

"What now?" said Elise.

The dog closed his eyes and sniffed.

"Smell that?" he said. "Giorgio's deep-pan pizza Margherita. We can share one on the way home. You can have the base and I'll have the toppings."

Elise gripped the dog's collar and explained in no uncertain terms that they were in town to find material for a bow tie, not to eat pizza.

"Ah, but look at the tablecloths, lassie."

Elise peered round the door of the pizzeria, which had about a dozen customers. It was a nice place with candles and concertina music, and the tables were covered by lovely green and yellow chequered tablecloths.

"Do you see what I see?" said the dog.

"Yes," said Elise. "But how does the bow tie factor into all of this?"

"Let's go in," said the dog. "I'll show you a trick I used to do in my heyday in Tobermory."

"In your what?"

"In my heyday. McAduddi was on top of the world back then. Ships were named for me, you know."

"Don't you think you're exaggerating just a bit?"

"Perhaps a little."

Papa Giorgio was a large man with a pencil moustache, and when he spotted the second-hand dog, he clapped his hands together and declared that the lovely doggy would have one of Giorgio's meatballs made using Mamma Giorgio's recipe, which was famed throughout Naples.

"And he'll have it free of charge! No need to pay."

Giorgio spoke so loudly that all his patrons

could hear.

"Without Mamma," said Giorgio, "there would have been no pizza and no pepperoni for Giorgio when he was a bambino. When I think of Mamma back in Napoli, my eyes start to water, but when I saw that chunky little doggy wagging its wonky tail, it was like the sun coming out."

Giorgio put a dish of three meatballs on the floor. The second-hand dog ate them in one gulp.

"The fat little doggy just loves Giorgio's meatballs!" laughed Giorgio. "They are the favourite of every dog in Napoli. Every night they sit in the moonlight and serenade my beloved mamma, because it's Mamma who came up with the recipe for Giorgio's meatballs. Mamma mia, you have made so many dogs so happy! It makes me well up, thinking about everything Mamma has done."

Giorgio took a picture of Mamma down from the wall and kissed it five times.

"No one in all of Napoli had a childhood like Giorgio, because Giorgio has the best mamma in the world. Let me get my concertina so I can play Mamma's favourite song."

Giorgio found his concertina and rallied his employees, three Italians from Tirana, who immediately got ready to sing along with Giorgio's oompah-oompah melody.

In fair old Napoli, where the sun always shines.
There lives a signora, a relative of mine.
Oh, Mamma, Mamma, my one true love.
Making lovely pizza, fit for the heavens above.
Oh, Mamma, Mamma, my one true love.
Making lovely pizza, fit for the heavens above.

The second-hand dog started coughing and staggering around the room.

People stared at him.

The second-hand dog's eyes rolled back and he fell onto his side, kicking his legs feebly a few times before getting back up again.

We sing all day in fair old Napoli.
We eat lovely pizza, very, very cheesy.
Oh, Mamma, Mamma, my one true love.
Making lovely pizza...

Giorgio stopped singing as he caught sight of the dog, which started coughing again, even more violently.

Giorgio told Elise he'd appreciate it if she removed her dog from his restaurant.

"Maybe my dog doesn't like Mamma's meatballs," said Elise.

"Are you crazy?" hissed Giorgio. "Everyone loves Mamma's meatballs."

The dog flopped down onto his stomach.

Elise crouched over him.

"Are you OK, Duddi?"

The dog stuck his tongue out and rolled his eyes.

"Urgh," he groaned, all the while instructing Elise out the corner of his mouth to wrap him in a tablecloth and carry him out of the pizzeria. If she could add another handful of meatballs into the bargain, all the better.

Elise looked at Giorgio, who moaned that his back was playing up again, all thanks to the dog.

"This is what you get for showing kindness. This would never have happened in Napoli, where the dogs are more grateful. No dogs in the whole world are more grateful than the ones in Napoli."

Elise said she was sorry for the trouble they had caused.

"But may I borrow a tablecloth?" she said. "To carry him home in? He's too sick to walk."

Giorgio clutched at his back.

"Just get him out of here," he groaned. "If Mamma could see me now, she would cry big salty tears. No one in the world cries like mamma mia."

❧

Ten minutes later Elise and the second-hand dog were strolling along Mysundegade. Elise had a chequered tablecloth under her arm, and the dog was walking at her side with a soup bone in his mouth.

That same evening, Elise went to see Miss Martini and her sewing machine. As so often before, Miss Martini was wearing a Chinese dress, so Elise put on an amber-coloured kimono that went with her hair, which had been twisted into a long plait. The second-hand dog lay on the sofa with his soup bone, and Miss Martini's favourite record played on the gramophone, with Jim Reeves singing so beautifully about love that Miss Martini asked Elise to dance. It wasn't the first time they had danced together – Miss Martini had actually taught Elise to dance the modern waltz and the tango, back when Elise had been so small she could just stand on Miss Martini's feet – but now they were almost the same height, they danced like a real couple, and when Jim sang *Don't forget a small moonbeam / Fold in lightly with a dream*, Miss Martini had to pause to wipe away a tear.

❧

Half an hour later, Elise snuck into their dimly lit flat on the fourth floor where her dad lay stretched out on the floor with his eyes closed. He was soaring on

Albinoni's flying carpet and didn't notice the girl with the yellow-chequered bow tie, even though it smelled intensely of pizza Margherita.

13

Since Christmas Eve was approaching, Elise's dad went down to Netto and bought four packets of raw marzipan. He was quite good with his hands, but it still took him all night to sculpt the Virgin Mary and baby Jesus surrounded by three Christmas elves and two reindeer. Some years there weren't any reindeer, and one year the Virgin Mary had been very small, which may have had something to do with the fact that Elise's dad kept eating the marzipan. When he was sculpting he always listened to the same music, a canon, which is a melody begun in different parts that overlap. Elise liked to think that Pachelbel, who composed the piece, had written the melody while eating marzipan.

As mentioned, Elise's dad always made the figures at night, so the music was very low because Elise was sleeping. Well, she usually was, but not this year. This Christmas Eve Eve she was wide awake, because she had been looking forward to this night since she had been up in the attic. All her old clothes, including the red Dickens dress bought in London several years ago, were in the attic, but it was not the Christmas dress that had given Elise her good idea – it was her dad's old hammock. Her dad had never used the hammock, which was made of thin cords and thick ropes strung together, but he had never been able to bring himself to get rid of it either. Elise was glad of that, because when she found the hammock, it occurred to her that her mental image of a hammock was not what a hammock was at all.

After carrying it down into her room, Elise gathered all the plants she could find in the flat. Her dad loved green plants, preferably of the very big and wild variety. He knew their Latin names and sang to them when he watered them. Most of the plants were in the hall, her dad's bedroom and the living room, but since he was making his marzipan figures in the

kitchen, the coast was clear for Elise to grab them.

Quick as a flash, she carried the plants into her room, and when she was done, she took the small stepladder and four hooks she had found in the toolbox and screwed them into the wooden panelling beneath the ceiling.

The second-hand dog, who rarely slept in his cardboard box now, instead making himself comfortable in Elise's bed, looked up at her.

"Are we doing something we shouldn't?"

Elise said it was a secret.

"I hope it doesn't have anything to do with me," said the dog, "because if I don't get my beauty sleep, I get very forgetful, and then things get left in the living room that no one wants to see."

Elise climbed down the ladder and sat next to the dog.

"We," she said, "are going on the most amazing journey."

"Journey?" said the dog. "It's the middle of the night. My legs are already asleep."

Elise smiled.

"Put this on while I finish up with the rubber plants, weeping fig and the rest of the rainforest."

The second-hand dog stared at the headband with the red feather in it.

"If anything's going on my head it's a nightcap."

"I'll be wearing a belt with sharp knives and a black revolver, and a mustard-yellow explorer's helmet which was once brown but has now faded so much in the sun that it's turned yellow. Feel how hot it is? That's because I've turned up the radiator."

"So that's why I smell like a gymnasium."

Elise smiled.

"It's over thirty degrees in here, but it'll be even hotter when we reach the rainforest."

Elise danced around to the music coming from the living room. She really liked Pachelbel, but she liked her idea even more, and even though it was past midnight, she was not in the least bit tired.

"You'll wear a gold chain around your neck to start, and then later we'll find out your name," she said.

The dog yawned.

"You know fine well what my name is, and we're not changing it. Look at my eyes. How do they look?"

"They're bloodshot."

"And that's because I'm exhausted."

"Why on earth are you exhausted?"

"I've been chasing a three-legged fly all day."

"Wow, how did that end?"

"It hasn't, yet. Back home in Scotland we say that a fly who pits itself against a dog is bound to lose a leg."

Elise scratched her neck.

"Let's see. What should we call you? You were born in the rainforest, you've never been outside of it and you hunt for your food. You could be called Wandering Feather, or Smelly Rabbit... or what about Limping Wolf?"

Not without some difficulty, the second-hand dog rolled over.

"I won't be Smelly Wolf or Limping Feather or anything else. My name's McAduddi. You won't take my pride from me. My family goes way back.

My great-great-great grandad made a living stealing chickens."

Elise clapped her hands.

"I know! You'll be called Dancing Dog."

"Dancing Dog?"

"It's important for a rainforest dog to have a name that says something about them."

"Well, maybe," the dog grumbled. "But I don't think Dancing Dog really does it. If I really have to have a rainforest name, I suggest Sleeping Dog, and while I'm thinking about it, there's a veal chop in the fridge I wouldn't be unhappy to see in my food bowl tomorrow."

"Dancing Dog it is," said Elise firmly.

Elise put her hands on her hips and grinned at the dog.

"This," she whispered, "is the beginning of the most dangerous journey of your life."

Elise put on her red shorts and favourite T-shirt with a picture of King Kong. She also wore her big winter boots and the faded explorer's helmet. Though it was night in the rainforest, she had a pair of binoculars around her neck – infrared binoculars that could see in the dark.

Elise was in the Amazon rainforest, but she wasn't alone, because she had Dancing Dog with her, a four-legged local who as well as being brave, also knew the area like the back of his paw.

Elise was armed with a dangerous knife, a very dangerous revolver and two packets of salty liquorice, and her task was to repair the suspension bridge over the extremely dangerous Amazon River. It wouldn't be easy, since the bridge wasn't finished, but that wasn't even the worst of it. The worst part was the night-time predators which made themselves heard when they closed on in their prey. The jaguar hunted at night, when it could be sure no one would see it, as did the scorpion and the tarantula, but they were nothing compared to the animal Elise feared most – the nine-metre-long snake they called the anaconda. It could grow to be so big it could eat ten ducks, one right after the other.

"But we have to be brave," said Elise to her companion.

"We can't see our own hands in front of our faces," said Dancing Dog, "and I don't trust the integrity of that suspension bridge."

Elise said they would have to move very carefully because if they put one foot wrong they might fall into the river below, and there were piranhas in the river capable of peeling a man quicker than a man could peel a banana.

A full moon the same colour as a blood orange hung in the sky over the bridge. For some reason this sight went well with the sounds from the rainforest, which were hollow and frightening.

Elise put an arm around Dancing Dog.

"You were born here. You should know what to do when you're in the middle of the rainforest surrounded by hungry predators and horrible tarantulas. What would someone who lived here do in this situation?"

"He'd go home to bed."

Elise clenched her teeth.

"But we need to secure that knot in the suspension bridge so it doesn't collapse, no matter the cost. We didn't travel this far to give up halfway. We mustn't forget our mission."

"So what now?"

"I wouldn't know, but I suggest you, as someone who lives here all the time, take the first step out onto the bridge."

"But I don't want to fall down to the piranhas," said Dancing Dog. "They'll need to find something else to eat. Like kibble."

Elise drew her knife.

"Be brave, Dancer," she said, "and follow me. If we are to go to our deaths, let's at least do it together."

"But I don't want to go to my death," said Dancing Dog. "I'm prepared to walk through fire and water, and to brave the local supermarket after four, but I'm not prepared to go to my death."

Soon they were out on the derelict suspension bridge, which swung alarmingly in the night wind. A harpy eagle screeched above their heads, and a howler monkey yowled somewhere in the rainforest.

Elise kneeled to tie a knot in the thick rope.

"Oh help," she said. "I think I saw a crocodile in the river below. It opened its huge mouth and gave me a hopeful smile."

"I saw it too," groaned Dancing Dog. "It was bigger than a chest freezer. How's about you empty your revolver into it?"

Elise frowned.

"I don't condone shooting defenceless animals and I'm not going to make an exception for this particular crocodile. He won't fancy someone like you for a midnight snack anyway. Come on, let's get moving while there's still light to see by."

Elise crawled out towards the middle of the bridge. It wasn't easy thanks to the sticky vines everywhere.

"I don't have to tell you,' she said, "that some of these plants are flesh-eating."

"I know," said Dancing Dog. "They'll eat it right from your hands."

"Stop," cried Elise. "Don't take another step!

There's a tarantula in front of me the size of a dinner plate. Can you get rid of it, Dancer?"

Dancer said he would try. After all, he had a lot of experience with dinner plates. He gripped the long knife between his teeth and closed in on the tarantula in five quick steps.

"Look out!" shouted Elise. "It might be some sort of horrible trick."

"I have my own tricks up my sleeve," said Dancing Dog. "One in particular is very cunning, and it helps tremendously that the whole bridge is shaking. The more I look at that disgusting bloodsucker, the more I shake, and look, it's losing its footing, it's about to fall over the edge. It's hanging by two legs over the abyss."

Elise stared at the tarantula clinging to the rope of the bridge.

"Say your prayers, ya wee beastie," said Dancing Dog.

Elise said she didn't think a tarantula could pray.

"I kind of feel sorry for it. Just because you happen to be a tarantula doesn't mean you don't deserve a little respect."

"True," said Dancing Dog, but it didn't stop him from kicking the tarantula in the shin. It lowered itself slowly into the abyss with a hideous screech.

"You're a true local," Elise said.

"We do know how to handle our insects," said Dancing Dog. "And if we carry on like this, there won't be a mayfly left by daybreak."

Five minutes later they had reached the far side of the rainforest.

They had crossed the derelict suspension bridge with their lives intact.

They sat down on a tree trunk for a well-deserved break.

"It's rough-going in this rainforest," said Elise, wiping the sweat from her brow. "How nice to find somewhere to rest our tired legs – and it's so comfy!"

Dancing Dog asked what the big snake that lived in the rainforest was called.

"An anaconda," said Elise. "It can grow to be nine metres long and as thick as a tree trunk. The anaconda is one big muscle and the most dangerous killer in the rainforest."

"And it'll eat anything?"

"So I hear," said Elise. "It eats animals and people and sometimes even cod livers."

"Does it have patterned skin?" asked Dancer.

"It's kind of speckled, with yellow, brown and green colouring."

"So a bit like this tree trunk we're sitting on."

Elise nodded.

"A lot like this tree trunk we're sitting on. Really quite a lot."

"Has it occurred to you," said Dancing Dog, "that what we're sitting on might not actually be a tree trunk at all?"

"What else would it be?"

"Well, it's sure as hell not a woodlouse."

Elise raised her torch and shone it on the tree trunk, which, right enough, was speckled yellow and green. Slowly she moved the light up to the end of the tree trunk, where two narrow eyes gleamed in the dark.

"If this is a tree trunk," said Dancing Dog, "I'm

a Pekinese, and unless I'm much mistaken, it's nine metres long."

"We'll soon find out," said Elise, pulling a ruler out of her back pocket.

"Well, aren't you well-prepared," said Dancer.

"You should never come to the rainforest without a ruler," said Elise, unfolding it to its full length.

She measured the tree trunk from end to end, and as it turned out, the tree trunk was exactly nine metres long.

"Can I say something?" said Dancing Dog.

"Of course, Dancing Dog."

"What we're sitting on has never been a tree trunk."

"No," said Elise. "And that's why we should sit still and be very brave. You need to be brave when you're in the jungle. In here you're all alone with the hole in your stomach."

"A hole?"

"Yep, a hole. Do you know what that hole's called?"

Dancing Dog said he didn't know.

"It's not called anything," said Elise, "but

sometimes you can feel it. You feel empty inside. Luckily I have something that can help."

Elise pulled a bag out of her pocket.

"Looks like salty liquorice," said Dancing Dog.

Elise nodded.

"You can get it sent to the jungle by airmail, it's a perfect mix of salty and sugary, and it helps against homesickness. Rachmaninoff ate it too."

Elise looked deep into Dancing Dog's eyes.

"There's something else we need to remember."

"What's that?"

"We need to remember planes take us home as well as away."

"Is that important?" asked Dancing Dog, and Elise said it was the most important thing in the world.

"And now it's time for us to go home."

They turned back the way they had come, and in the middle of the suspension bridge, Elise found a string hanging down from the night sky. And so it was that they flew home across the rainforest, the dog and the girl, holding the moon on a string.

14

Elise and Aunt Fie had parked Fie's car at the station in Klampenborg and were now sitting in an old horse-drawn carriage on their way to Hermitage Hunting Lodge in Dyrehaven forest park.

It was a bitterly cold February day, and Fie was wrapped up in a jet-black gorilla fur coat with a luminous belt. Elise was wearing a padded coat, a scarf, gloves and a woolly hat. Fie had brought a Thermos of hot chocolate and a bottle of soapy water so she could blow soap bubbles while they trundled down the forest path.

She nudged Elise, who was sitting with her shoulders slumped and a distant expression. That aside, the combination of the sound of the horse's hooves, the grey sky and the bare, black trees was

really something.

Elise and Fie often went on trips by horse-drawn carriage, but never in February, and today it was like they had winter to themselves.

"It's like we're the only people in the whole world," said Fie. "Riding through the black forest and sending smoke signals up in the form of soap bubbles. Actually, scratch that, we're sailing – sailing between tropical islands!"

Fie started singing.

"*They said come sail away, come sail away, come sail away with me*. That's my favourite song. Do you recognise it?"

Elise said she didn't.

"I sang it to you all the time when your mum was pregnant."

Elise shrugged.

"I only remember Albinoni."

Fie nudged Elise's shoe with her boot.

"You look a bit glum, love."

"Do I?"

Fie nodded.

"Yes, and that won't do, because this is when the tide starts to turn. Right here and now. Can't you see it? Don't you hear it? That's why we're here, to revel in it."

"To revel in what?"

Fie blew a load of soap bubbles up into the air.

"The return of the light. I love the second of February, everything explodes – you can still smell winter, but you can tell spring's on the way. When you stick your head out the window, the city smells of ash, seawater, wet wood and sweet pastry. That's why the second of February is like no other day."

Elise looked up at the sky.

"My dog's gone."

Fie put the bottle of soapy water away and moved closer to Elise.

"Gone where?"

Elise shrugged.

"He's just gone. It was so strange, because just before he disappeared, I woke up during the night and saw him looking at me, and then it was like he was getting smaller and smaller. Maybe it was a dream, but I do remember, quite clearly, that he said something to me."

Fie turned Elise's head so they could look each other in the eye.

"Dogs disappear, and then they show up again. How long's he been gone?"

"Ten days," said Elise, looking up at the sky. "I've been out looking for him every night. I go out with my head torch after Dad's fallen asleep. There are a lot of stray dogs in Vesterbro, you know. For some reason I thought he might be up near Central Station, but he wasn't. He's nowhere."

"You've been walking around town at night?"

"From twelve to four."

Fie leaned forward and clenched her fists.

"You can't do that! There are all sorts of weirdos wandering around at night!"

Elise nodded.

"Yeah, I know, but none of them have seen him.

I thought I saw him one night, I called his name and ran after him, and we made it all the way to the cemetery at the end of Enghavevej."

"Elise, please tell me you weren't running around in Vestre Cemetery."

"I thought he'd run inside, but it wasn't him. It was another dog. Then I went home via St Matthew's Church, where there was a light on. There were two girls sitting shivering in the church. I think they were from Africa. I told them my dog was missing, and we prayed he'd come back. I even prayed to Mr Mortensen, even though I know deep down Duddi's gone to Aberdeen. That's what he told me in my dream. He also said that now the big band would march through town with drums and bagpipes."

Elise found a tissue in Fie's bag.

"I don't mind crying, but there's always so much snot involved."

Fie put a hand on Elise's arm.

"Dogs wander off. It's in their nature."

Elise took a deep breath.

"Have you forgotten what it means when a dog says they're going to Aberdeen? You're the one who told me. We were on Værnedamsvej having brunch."

Fie took Elise's hand.

"Look at me. You know I love you more than anyone else on earth, but if the worst has happened, I suggest you take your big mental eraser and rub that dog out of your head. Life goes on, even after a second-hand dog."

Elise clenched her teeth and counted slowly and very clearly.

"My dog was my best friend, how can I just erase him? I had the moon on a string when I was with him."

Fie pulled Elise to her.

"You're a lucky spud. I've never had the moon on a string."

Elise took another deep breath.

"Dad once said that when he played Albinoni he had the world in the palm of his hand. Me and my dog had the world in the palms of our hands too, though sometimes we also had our tails between our legs. He was always there. He never disappeared. Until now. The best thing was we could talk about anything. I know it sounds strange, considering he was a dog."

"I'll say."

"What?"

Fie shrugged.

"I just mean it was a bit odd he could only talk to you. I remember sitting outside your grandma's mill trying to engage him in conversation, but all he'd say was woof. To be completely honest, he sounded just like any other doggy."

Elise glared daggers at her.

"That's because he didn't *want* to speak. When you left he said loads. He wouldn't talk to just anyone. Neither would you."

"All I'm saying is no matter how much you loved him, you need to keep things in perspective."

"I don't know what you mean."

"Just don't make him into something more than he was."

"You think I am?"

"A bit."

"Oh, just stop, will you? We flew over the rainforest, we went to Giorgio's pizzeria, we hunted vampires and ate rice pudding until we felt sick, he got me material for Dad's Christmas present, he taught me to sing sea shanties and told me how bagpipes were invented... we had the moon on a string. What more could you want?"

Fie put an arm around Elise.

"I'm on your side, Lissi, never think otherwise. You say your dog could talk? Fine, he could talk. All that stuff about Scotland and Tobermory? Fine. The *Highland Park* whisky thing? Fine."

Elise wriggled free.

"You and your fines. Nothing's fine. There's a big difference between something being fine and something being true, and you shouldn't talk to me like I'm a baby."

"Sorry, I didn't mean to. Honestly, Elise, you know that."

"You know nothing, Fie. Nothing."

"Clearly."

"Yes, clearly."

Elise sat down on the opposite seat.

"A year ago I got so angry I held my breath for so long you drove me to the emergency room, but I won't do that now, and that's because it doesn't matter to me what you believe and what you don't. But I'd never heard of a whisky called *Highland Park* until I met my dog, there was never any of it in the flat, and I'm not coming to the festival on Saturday."

"Can I say something?"

"I don't want to celebrate anything, especially not stupid Candlemas."

Fie lowered her voice.

"I'm not trying to play the adult or to be clever or anything, because by heavens there's nothing wrong with having an active imagination. What would we do without our imaginations? There's nothing more important. Without them we'd be nothing. The world begins and ends with people who tell stories, let their imaginations run riot and enjoy themselves."

Elise answered by closing her eyes, taking a deep breath and holding it.

Fie stared at her.

"Breathe, Elise. Please breathe. You're scaring me, breathe, we're in the middle of a forest."

Fie shook Elise, but Elise knew she could hold her breath for several minutes, so she just clamped her mouth even more tightly closed and squeezed her eyes shut.

"Stop it, Elise. I won't put up with this. You're being a pain. Breathe!"

Elise gave Fie a sharp look and said she didn't want to hear another word about having an active imagination.

The driver turned and said all children had active imaginations. Fie asked him to be quiet and see to his horse.

Elise looked at the bracelet she had got from Potifar's ship. It was dark blue.

"There is one thing I believe."

"What?"

"What they say about the caliph's bracelet. I believe in what it can do. One hundred per cent."

Fie flapped her hand dismissively.

"Well, good."

Elise sighed.

"You can see for yourself it's blue. It's not changed colour because we're sitting in a horse-drawn carriage or because it's the second of February. Potifar got the bracelets from India, so he must know what he's talking about."

Fie propped her chin up on her hands.

"I shop in a second-hand shop and don't have any clothes that haven't also been worn by someone else, but I still think you should take what Potifar tells you about the things in his shop with a pinch of salt."

Elise shook her head.

"Dad says the caliph's bracelets were made in a factory in Ballerup. As if he knows the first thing about it, but anyway, it doesn't matter to me whether they were made in Ballerup, Bombay or Karlsruhe. I just know they work."

Fie patted Elise on the knee.

"Of course they work."

"Stop humouring me."

Fie leaned back and looked up at the sky.

"Then let's talk about something else, you've always said you like Candlemas more than any other festival, and we had an agreement, you know."

"We did?"

"Yes, we did. You were going to bring your new telescope, which you got for Christmas from – oh, how about that? – Potifar, and we were going to go up to the roof and look at the stars."

"The telescope's not new," said Elise. "It's second-hand. Everything in Potifar's shop is second-hand. That's what I like about it. It's good value. Like spending time with Great-Grandad."

Fie handed Elise another tissue.

"How does your Great-Grandad come in to all this?"

"I called him and told him my dog was probably

dead and that I was heartbroken."

"What did he say?"

"He said one of the other old people at the care home had eaten his egg sandwich. We agreed you sometimes lose what you love most."

Fie nodded.

"But it was a great present, the telescope, even if it is a bit battered."

Elise looked up at the winter sky, aware of two crystalline tears rolling down her cheeks. She had been deliriously happy when she unwrapped the telescope. It had been a wonderful Christmas Eve with Miss Martini, Grandma, Great-Grandad, the checkout lady from Netto, Potifar and Mrs Potifar, who was actually called Rita. Aunt Fie and Elise's dad had also been there, of course, and last but not least, McAduddi with his Santa hat on. They had walked around the Christmas tree twenty-four times, and Miss Martini had spoken Chinese, and Great-Grandad had told the story about the time he'd been let out. Everything had been great, everyone had been happy, no one had put a foot wrong, apart from Elise's dad, who had trodden in the rice pudding when they were dancing around Great-Grandad singing *We all live in a yellow submarine*.

When Elise thought about that Christmas Eve, the memory was bathed in honey-coloured light.

It had been that good.

🐾

The horse-drawn carriage stopped at the Hermitage Hunting Lodge and Fie and Elise got out to stretch their legs. The driver said something about the deer grazing on the lawn, and shortly afterwards they set off again.

On the way back, Fie asked whether Elise fancied a budget holiday somewhere where the sun was shining and the food was terrible.

"What, with a swimming pool and all that?"

"Something like that."

"Meh."

"Or we could just go to that Italian supermarket... you know, SuperMarco. It's up to you."

Fie's 2CV always had trouble starting when it was frosty. Luckily there were always some nice people around to give it a push.

Fie and Elise drove out to Langelinje, where they sat for half an hour watching containerships and bundled-up people eating hotdogs.

Fie said dogs didn't live forever, and Elise said she knew that.

Then she got out the car and gave it a push.

❖

The sun was just starting to set when she let herself into the dark flat on Mysundegade. Elise had never minded being home alone. Being alone had nothing to do with other people, it was possible to feel alone even when standing in line at Netto. In the flat it was different, it was always nice to be there even when you were alone. Sometimes you could hear the sound of other people's lives. But today the flat felt empty, as if there was nothing in it.

Even though Elise had promised her dad she would dust and hoover, she sat down on the window seat with her head against the wall. Her dad was playing his violin in Fisketorvet shopping centre and had promised to bring something nice home with him.

Elise found the five bike lights that still worked and positioned them around the living room. Then she put the recording of the Russian choir on the gramophone. The serious men from St Petersburg still sounded like they were singing about a dog who was about to be christened.

Elise went out into the hall to fetch the feather duster, but got lost in thought in front of the speaker. She had never noticed it before, but the music had a door you could open, and suddenly she was standing in front of the fat men with the sad voices. The choir was in a church, and the singers had been standing there for so long that cobwebs hung from their robes. They didn't seem bothered when Elise started dusting them, and when she was done, she sat down on the floor and looked up at the enormous dome, at the snow falling onto it in small white patches. But it wasn't snow, it was pieces of paper, torn-up letters and tiny fragments of Brazilian stamps.

FINAL

CHAPTER

The Candlemas festival was something of a tradition in the area of Vesterbro from Tove Ditlevsens Plads to Saxogade, and from Saxogade to Enghavevej. Businesses stayed open until late at night, which wasn't unusual in itself, but on this evening, they were lit by coloured lights and sparkling torches. In St Matthew's Church they served baguette and minestrone soup as cheerful organ music played, the notes suspended in the air like snowflakes across the neighbourhood.

During Candlemas this part of town was closed to cars and the streets were full of people having fun and eating burgers, shawarma, apple pancakes and pizza – when they weren't shopping at the flea market extending from the church down to Valdemarsgade.

Here you could buy everything for a reasonable price: kitchenware, Moroccan cushions, children's toys, standard lamps and blue triangular shelving units.

The Candlemas festival was a light in the dark of winter.

In the church vestibule the queue for the soup table was twenty people long, so the volunteers were busy. One of them was Elise's dad, who was giving the priest, the checkout lady from Netto and the verger a hand with the soup tureen. They had white aprons on, and Elise's dad was looking very fetching in his chequered bow tie which smelled of pizza Margherita.

Elise's grandma and Miss Martini had gone down to the flea market to look for a plastic tray for making ice cubes, and Elise's great-grandad was sitting in the gardens feeding breadcrumbs to the sparrows.

All Elise really wanted was to go home, but her dad had spent all day making soup with the checkout lady, and Elise didn't want to spoil the festival for him. She had also agreed to meet Aunt Fie at nine.

Elise really liked St Matthew's Church, which

was really old and really big. It smelled of nutmeg and had enough room for a thousand people. When her dad wasn't playing at a wedding or funeral, they went to the church and listened to the hymns while they ate the last of the morning rolls. Elise had been christened at St Matthew's Church, but when she thought about her christening, she was reminded of another christening – when she had christened her dog in the name of her mum, Potifar and Aunt Fie. Back then Elise had decided her dog would be called Prince Valiant. But that hadn't been his name. He had already had a name, because he had already had a life.

"Such is life," whispered Elise. "Such is life."

Her dad had asked her to help cut more bread. He said nothing in the world went together better than warm baguette, hot minestrone soup and good old Buxtehude.

"What sort of a name is that?"

Her dad said he'd had a hamster called Buxtehude.

"Here, have some soup. I'll put some colour in your cheeks."

Elise said she wasn't hungry.

"Is there a reason you're wearing sunglasses?"

"I'm wearing sunglasses because I want to wear sunglasses."

Elise's dad pulled her deeper into the church.

"I'm sad about the dog too."

"Are you?"

"Of course I am. He was a bit odd, but he was a nice dog, and that's why I thought maybe we could get a new one. A puppy from an actual kennels. How about it?"

Elise leaned towards her dad.

"Thanks," she said. "But I don't want a new dog. I'm off to find Aunt Fie. We agreed to meet in front of the bicycle repair shop on Valdemarsgade."

Elise's dad took her hand.

"Wow, you're getting big. I swear your hand's grown in the night. But never mind that. The point is, I hate seeing you so sad."

Elise shrugged.

"I'll get over it."

"You're a brave girl."

"I don't want to be brave. I'm nothing."

"You're the most important person in my life, but you have to stop wandering around town in the middle of the night. I hope we can agree on that, hm?"

Elise turned away from her dad.

"Alright, who squealed?"

"Elise, they weren't squealing, they just care about you. We all care about you. Not just your Aunt Fie and I, but Grandma, Great-Grandad, old Miss Martini and Potifar too."

"Did you tell Potifar I've been out looking for my dog at night?"

Elise's dad spoke through clenched teeth.

"He's been keeping watch on the corner every night since he heard."

Elise's dad put his face in his hands.

"For goodness sake, Elise, what were you thinking? What's going on in that head of yours?"

Elise put an arm around her dad.

"Sorry, I don't know what I was thinking, but I'm

done looking, I promise. I won't do it again."

Elise's dad clenched his fist. Elise did the same and they bumped them together. They did that sometimes, but they had never actually discussed what it meant.

Elise's dad kissed her on the cheek.

"Tell Fie to call me when you reach the bike shop."

Aunt Fie was waiting where they had arranged. She looked great in her long black coat and the ring of candles that sat like a crown on her head. If it hadn't been for the green trainers, she would have looked like the Statue of Liberty.

"Had your fill of organ music?"

Elise took her sunglasses off.

"Yes, I prefer Russian choral singing."

"Why's that?"

"Because it has a door you can go through."

Fie nodded.

"And where do you come out if you go through that door?"

"Home."

Fie massaged her temples as she chivvied Elise along. Elise grumbled that her nose was running.

"Well, 'tis the season and all that," said Fie. "And it has to be said, you *really* look the part."

"How else would I look?"

"Count your blessings you don't look like your Great-Grandad. Things might still go that way. You have more in common that you think. You're both equally headstrong, at any rate."

Elise said nothing, just stared into space.

Fie looked at her.

"Anyone home?"

Elise said she was hungry.

Fie smiled.

"And that's why we're going to get hotdog baguettes. We've earned something unhealthy. I'll just call your dad and tell him where we are. It's amazing how many people are out. You'd think the whole world had come to Vesterbro, but the smell, Lissi, there's nothing bad about that."

Elise nodded. She was right about that, the smell of fried food, Coca-Cola and petrol. It didn't get better than that. The only thing that might have improved it was a faint waft of old cheese.

Elise and Fie bought their hotdogs in Enghave Plads. They stood in line for half an hour, and now they were headed up to the roof. It was a clear and frosty evening with a pale blue Milky Way and a few determined stars.

"Do you think we'll be able to see all the way to Pluto with your new telescope?" said Aunt Fie.

Elise said that according to Potifar, you could see all the way to the first star God put in the sky. Potifar was very liberal with that sort of information, and as mentioned, the telescope wasn't new, but if they were lucky, they would be able to see the mountains on the moon.

Soon afterwards they were in front of the flats on

Mysundegade. Fie called Elise's dad to tell him where they were.

He wanted to talk to Elise, who took the phone.

"Can we meet in half an hour in front of the church?"

Elise didn't have a chance to answer.

The sound came as if from everywhere at once, perhaps mostly from above, and it was so intense that Elise stumbled into the wall.

It started deep, like the horn of a steamship on the open ocean. Then other instruments joined in, the sound building and building, and when the drums kicked in, there was no doubt. The music made the people at the flea market, the hotdog stand and in the church vestibule stop what they were doing, and when Elise and Fie made it down to the street corner, they could see what it was.

The band came walking up Istedgade, sixty men wearing kilts, boots, blue uniform jackets and black bearskin hats, playing bagpipes and drums. The drum major came first, and the sound that followed him could be heard all over Vesterbro.

Elise and Fie stood hand in hand, staring at the huge band as it marched past with all due pomp and circumstance. There were drums and bagpipes, including a bass drum with *Tobermory Highland Guards* written on it.

The band was heading for Enghavevej. Many of the people in the side streets followed the marching Scots, but not Elise. She walked quickly to her building and went up to the fourth floor, where she shut herself in the flat, found her telescope and carried it up the kitchen stairs.

It was freezing cold up on the roof, but Elise clenched her teeth and positioned the telescope so it was pointing in the right direction, towards Pluto. Elise hadn't had the telescope very long, but long enough that she could get a clear picture of what she wanted to look at.

She heard the door to the roof open and close behind her.

"I thought you'd be up here," said Fie, collapsing into

one of the wicker chairs. "I'm still all of a tizzy though."

"You probably took the stairs too quickly," said Elise.

Fie got up and went over to Elise.

"Look at me, Lissi, and tell me what's going on. Did you see the bass drum? Did you see what was written on it?"

Elise turned the telescope.

"Yes, I saw it."

"We need to talk about this. I can't stand not talking about it."

"Not now."

"What are you looking for?"

"Pluto," said Elise. "They say if you point your telescope at Pluto, you can see your heart's desire."

"Did Potifar tell you that?"

"No, my dog did."

Fie leaned closer to Elise.

"Is your heart's desire a star or a planet?"

Elise looked up at the moon's honey-yellow face with its satisfied smile.

"This," she said, "is an old second-hand telescope, and it can't actually see that far, but I can see a plane coming in to land at the airport, and it's yellow with a Brazilian flag on its wing."

Fie didn't say anything, just took a deep breath and put her arms around Elise, rocking her back and forth to the sound of drums and bagpipes, which grew fainter and fainter until finally it faded into the black night.

And so you might think that this is where the story ends, but it's not, because the next day it started over, with Elise telling her mum about the day in October she visited the animals' paradise and bought a second-hand dog.

Bjarne Reuter is a veritable literary institution in Denmark. A feature of almost every Dane's childhood, Reuter's writing encompasses not only humorous stories for children, but also young adult novels, crime novels and more. He has won numerous prizes including twice being a Hans Christian Andersen Award finalist.

Kirsten Raagaard was born in Kastrup, Denmark. Her first job was in an advertising company but by the early 1970's she had published her first illustrated children's short story. Although she continues to illustrate books, she now also enjoys writing her own picture books. She was nominated for the Nordic Children's Book Prize in 2002.

Siân Mackie completed her MSc in Literary Translation as a Creative Practice in 2013 at Edinburgh University and now enjoys translating everything from user manuals and medical texts to biographies and children's literature from all three Scandinavian languages.